BREAKING THE HABIT

REBEL INK BOOK 1

SUSAN HARRIS

Originally published as Kindle Vella Episodes

Cover Design by: Gem Promotions
Typography by: Gem Promotions

PROLOGUE

Rhys

THE MUSIC WAS POUNDING SO hard that the walls shook when Rhys put the palm of his hand on them to steady himself. The techno music made his head hurt but the girl he'd met at the hotel bar with lip gloss that tasted of raspberries had promised him a wild night and he couldn't stay cooped up in the hotel room all night.

It was suffocating to be around all the happy couples. Usually, Luna would be all for hitting a party with him but since she and the tattoo artist had hooked up, Luna was more about her boy and less about the party lifestyle. Jameson was in domestic bliss with Sinéad, and Declan...

Well, the less said about that the better.

Rhys fumbled his way to the kitchen, snagging another beer even though he knew he was three beers past his limit. He needed to block out some of the shit in his head, and just feel numb, forgetting all the shit he couldn't seem to get passed.

Why are you such a colossal fuck up?

Putting the bottle to his lips, Rhys drained half, felt his stomach roll, and had to shut his eyes to stop the room from spinning.

Jesus Christ, he just wanted to ache in his chest to subside.

"Hey, babe, you look like you could use a little pick me up."

Rhys opened his eyes to see raspberry lip-gloss girl in front of him, dressed only in jeans and a red lace bra. She smiled at him, then trailed fingers down the slope of her breast before she pulled a clear plastic bag with white power in it. He'd been to enough parties to know cocaine when he saw it but he'd never dabbled in drugs.

His brain was already all kinds of fucked up and adding drugs wouldn't help.

Rhys let the girl drag him toward the living room. There was a blonde girl lying on the coffee table, naked from the waist up, and some varsity-looking jock snorting coke off her tits before yanking her up and grinding against her up against the nearest wall.

Raspberry lip-gloss unclasped her bra, her breasts

spilling out, and then she was laying down on the coffee table, looking up at him. Opening the plastic bag, she poured a line of cocaine along the swell of one of her breasts and crooked a finger at him.

There was no way Rhys was in any condition to be making sound decisions and he took a step back, preparing to just leave this goddamn house in some Manchester housing estate.

Ya, great idea, genius. Head back to the hotel where your best friend is banging your sister.

Before Rhys could stop himself, he was down on his knees, lowering his face to this girl's flesh and inhaling the powder. His mind felt like it was being split open, then the girl rubbed some cocaine on her lips and got up to kiss him.

He felt euphoric, weightless. Exactly what he'd been wanting to feel for the longest time. There were lips and hands and lots of touching, as the ache in his chest dissipated. Suddenly the music was the best thing he'd ever heard in his life.

Climbing to the back of the living room couch Rhys whooped and danced, throwing off his leather jacket and feeling free. His head was so fogged that he couldn't hear his own thoughts but it was like emerging from the water and being cleansed.

Then, Rhys was hit with a wave of dizziness, lost his footing, and fell backwards with so much force that he went right through the window, glass smashing around him, and when he landed, it was on a bed of concrete and glass, his arms and face stinging.

Rhys barely heard the screams coming from the house as he tried to sit up but just couldn't muster the strength to do it. Instead, Rhys looked up at the opaque sky and laughed at the way his skin burned from the cuts of glass and when he heard the wail of a siren, Rhys closed his eyes and welcomed the darkness.

CHAPTER ONE

Rhys

Thirty Five Days Later

Rhys kept his eyes firmly on the scenery that blurred by as the car headed back home. It was bad enough that the band mandated he go to a 'retreat' to deal with his mental health, but Rhys had known that everyone was worried he was an addict. In truth, he'd been an absolute idiot and fallen through a window after doing drugs for the first time ever.

When he'd woken in the hospital the next morning, he wasn't surprised his sister, and his band manager Andi were standing at the foot of the bed, his best friend and lead singer of their band Heartache

Melody sitting a little closer to Rhys, his arms folded across his chest and his eyes closed like he was sleeping.

Rhys had reached out, his mouth dry as all hell, knocked over the jug of water and alerted the other two he was awake. Andi glared at him with an achingly familiar expression, like she was seething with anger, but her eyes were red from crying.

"You're a fucking total idiot, you know that right?"

Rhys rubbed his temple, then glanced down at the vast array of cuts on his arms. It wasn't pretty. Pulling himself up in the bed, Rhys had realized that he'd also gotten a little slashed on his torso. There was a bandage over a patch of flesh just under his ribs and when he touched it, pain made him curse.

"You had a shard of glass embedded that they had to surgically remove. You were so off your head that you didn't even realize it was stuck in you. What the hell were you thinking, Rhys?"

Rhys had ignored her, turning his head away and looking anywhere but at Andi or Declan for that matter, but Andi stormed into his line of sight. "Don't you bloody ignore me. You could have killed yourself and you don't get to give me attitude right now. Cocaine, Rhys. Cocaine!" Andi's words had come out hissed, not that he blamed her; he'd been a stupid asshole. Yet, Rhys couldn't just say he was sorry and let it all go.

"Don't pretend you care, Andi. Just leave me the hell alone."

It was then Andi started shouting about going to rehab and sorting himself out and Rhys had told her to go fuck herself, but Declan told Rhys if he didn't go for a mental health break, then he was out of the band.

It was the only reason Rhys had agreed to their stupid plan, despite arguing that he hadn't even used coke before, and he wasn't inclined to do it again. Once he was discharged from the hospital, Rhys hadn't been left alone for a single minute, until Andi and Declan had dropped him off at the super private, middle of nowhere retreat.

He had done his mandatory thirty days and been discharged. Andi had been waiting for him when he was released and had frowned when Rhys had thrown his bag in the back seat, then climbed into the passenger side and not said a word. He knew he was being childish, but, Rhys had spent the last thirty days talking to strangers about himself and he was tired of talking.

Well, to be fair, the first five days he'd said nothing in the mandatory groups but that wasn't the point.

"Mam and Dad are dying to see you. They wanted to make sure I told you that you could come and stay with them for a while. I think mam really wants to make sure you've been looking after yourself while you've been away. I told her that you were staying with me and Declan, but we'd drop in tomorrow or the day after, once you've settled."

Rhys wanted to go back and be smothered by his parents like he wanted a lobotomy and he sure as shit didn't want to become Andi and Declan's roommate.

"I'm not staying with you, Andi. I'm going home to my own bed." Rhys said as he looked at her for the first time since they left the retreat in Kildare.

Andi glanced at him, her grip on the steering wheel tightening. "I don't think you should spend your first few days by yourself, Rhys. Stay with me and Declan, it's no hassle."

"I'd rather go through another pane of glass then bunk up with you and Dec. I've spent the last thirty days under constant surveillance and I just want to be alone, Andi. Just leave me be alone."

Rhys tried not to feel bad when Andi flinched when he mentioned falling through the window, but Rhys really didn't want to see the hurt in her eyes. He was doing that a lot lately, hurting her, and it made him feel terrible because he and Andi used to be so close.

Maybe the therapist was right and his insecurities started when Rhys had made friends with Declan and then Declan and Andi had become friends and Rhys felt that he was the unnecessary one in their little trio.

And it wasn't like the retreat had been so bad. The having to talk was utter shite. But, they had lots of little recreational rooms, like a gym, a tv room, and a music room, where Rhys had spent a lot of his time. They had a baby grand piano and it was refreshing to be able to sit there alone and play to his heart's content, indulging himself in the secret he'd been hiding for years because he knew he wasn't as good Andi or Declan.

Not a single person knew that Rhys could actually sing.

Andi had known he could hold a tune before his voice broke, but when it did, Rhys had been so self-conscious that he'd pretended to be bad...even using a fake singing voice so no one would suspect and it was never mentioned again.

Rhys had spent hours in that music room, just playing until his fingers ached and his throat was sore. It had been so bad one night, he'd asked one of the nursing staff if someone could get him some Tanora and honey to soothe his vocal cords. He'd played music that wasn't Heartache Melody songs, just songs he liked to listen to in his alone time.

It wasn't long before he started to amass a crowd, mostly in the evenings, when activities were finished for the day and people were looking for other shit to do besides be alone with their thoughts. Rhys didn't mind the audience, especially since there was little chance of any of the other stars sharing videos of Rhys singing and playing piano when according to their socials' they themselves were on a beach in Bali or swimming with pigs in the Bahamas.

Rhys closed his eyes and sighed, feeling the weight of Andi's stare on him. He'd learned enough in therapy to know that he missed Andi, missed the bond they had before things got twisted in his head, and he missed having someone he could call and just say he wasn't feeling great.

It wasn't her fault that things were strained between them.

Nope...that was all his doing.

"Rhys."

Prying his eyes open, Rhys turned slightly to look at his sister and blinked when he noticed just how tired she looked. They were stopped at traffic lights as Andi chewed on her bottom lip before she spoke.

"I really do think you should stay with someone for a few days. If you can't stand to be around me, or the parents, then maybe Luna or Jamie would come stay with you."

Rhys sighed loudly, shaking his head. "I don't need a babysitter, Andi. I had enough of that to last me a lifetime. I just want some space. I'm not going to party or go on a bender now that I'm out. I just wanna chill for a few days before I have to deal with everyone watching me. Can you just give me that. Please?"

Andi looked like she wanted to argue, however, she drove her car to his little bungalow, not saying anything as Rhys muttered his thanks, got out, and grabbed his bag from the backseat.

"Rhys?"

Rhys ducked his head into the car when his sister called him.

"You'll call me, if you need anything?"

"Sure." Rhys told her as he closed the door and headed up the pathway to his house, stepping inside, closing the door, dropping his bag on the ground, and leaning against the door. The silence was almost deafening.

CHAPTER TWO

Rhys

Rʜʏs ʙᴜsɪᴇᴅ himself tidying up his little haven, even though he expected his mother had been over and fussed about the place. His stash of booze had been emptied out, and no evidence of his excessive drinking remained. Rhys himself knew it was a bit much but the thoughts in his head were sometimes so fucking loud that he had to drown them out, sometimes by necking a bottle of vodka.

When he'd been asked in his therapy sessions about why he drank so much or why he decided to try drugs, Rhys hadn't had a very good answer. It felt stupid, telling this complete stranger that sometimes his thoughts overwhelmed him and he wanted to shut them off. That he wasn't sure if he was jealous that his sister and his best friend were now a thing, or if he was just angry that it felt like he had to share.

And that made him feel like a prize prick.

Ever since Declan and Andi had fallen out, Rhys had been able to spend time with Andi and vent about the band, or spend time with Dec and vent about his family. Now, it just felt like wherever he went, they were there, together. Somehow his stupid brain hadn't figured out that by tricking Andi into becoming their manager, it meant his sister was always gonna be part of the band's business. Now, with the two of them dating, Rhys felt confused.

Rhys huffed out a breath and went to take a shower, hoping to pass away the time in some useful way instead of mulling over all the shit decisions he'd been making lately. After his shower, Rhys pulled on a grey pair of sweatpants and headed to the fridge to see if there was any food, smiling when he saw it was packed.

Making himself a sandwich, it made him consider that his diet before the retreat had been mainly a mixture of junk food and alcohol. He knew he'd lost weight, but after three meals day for thirty days and daily gym workouts, he'd started to feel more like himself than he had in a long time.

After brewing a cup of tea, Rhys went into the small living room and plonked down in front of the TV, turning on some random cooking competition for background noise. He glanced around for his phone, then realized that Andi probably still had it, after Declan confiscated it in the hospital.

Anger bubbled inside of him and Rhys closed his eyes to calm himself. He knew that his phone was full of one-night stands and party people who Rhys was better off without and he himself had planned a cleanse of his contacts once he had gotten home, but this was ridiculous.

A memory struck him then, of the night before he'd gone off to the retreat.

"Where are you going, Rhys?"

"Fuck off, Declan. You're not my father." Rhys tossed back at him, grabbing his phone and keys, ready to head out his parent's front door. There was a party going on in the city and if he was to be sent off on this useless retreat, then he was going to bid his freedom goodbye in style.

Declan blocked his path, holding out his hand. "Gimmie your phone. The same idiots inviting you to a party are the same idiots that left you bleeding when you went through that window. You're not stupid, Rhys. They aren't your friends."

Rhys felt his lips curve into a sneer. "You wanna be my friend now, Dec? That's rich. And here I thought you'd dropped me because you got what you wanted. I mean, no need to be friends with me now you're fucking my sister."

Rhys heard his mother suck in a breath as Declan

grabbed him by the collar, his face flushed red with anger. Rhys wanted Declan to hit him, wanted to feel the pain, and yet, Declan just held him as his mother took the phone from Rhys hands, and then Declan shoved him back, shaking his head.

"You keep pushing my buttons, Rhys, and so help me god, I will lay you out. You don't get to speak about Andi like that. She's still your sister, no matter how you feel about me right now."

Rhys brushed the wrinkles off his t-shirt. "Awh look at ya, Dec, playing the hero...does it make ya feel fucking special, having a band full of misfits you can say you saved?"

Declan shook his head, a frown creasing his brows. "I dunno who you are right now, Rhys."

A snort escaped Rhys and he smirked. "Maybe this is who I've always been, Dec. The fuckboy of the band, arrogant and selfish. Now get out of my way."

The air that was already charged seemed to crackle with tension as Rhys went to step around Declan, but his mam blocked the way a stern look on her face that was unusual for the women who gave her kids the space to make their own decisions and their own mistakes.

Mabel Collins spoke, her tone firm. "I've made dinner and you are gonna sit down and eat because you look like you're fading away. I don't know what's happening to you, luv, but it's killing me."

The pain in her voice almost broke Rhys, tears threatening to spill from his eyes. Part of him wanted to *rebel, to walk past his mam and into the night. Instead he sat down at the table for dinner.*

His mam watched every mouthful he swallowed, raising her brows when he pushed the food around his plate so Rhys ate every bite even though it make him feel queasy.

Rhys had known he had been baiting Declan, trying to incite him to violence and he had caused the rift between his best friend and himself. Hell, he knew he was still pushing Andi away.

"The road to forgiveness is not an easy road, Rhys. But you have to learn to forgive yourself first. Then and only then can you seek forgiveness from those you have hurt."

Rhys knew the advice was good, yet, he didn't think he was ready to forgive himself for being a dickhead. He needed to figure out who he was and who he wanted to be. He needed to see why being Rhys Collins scared him and see if he could survive the ninety days challenge set out by his therapist to find his way back to being someone he wasn't ashamed of.

"Ninety days," She'd said with a smile. "Ninety days of no drinking, no partying, no sex. None of the crutches you use to hide away from being you. Use the time to keep a clear head and make amends. That's my challenge to you, Rhys."

Jesus Christ, he wanted a drink so badly.

Not that he was an alcoholic. He'd managed the thirty days without so much as a drop but then again, he'd been so busy, routine and structure and music, that it hadn't bothered him. However, right now, stuck here in the silence, Rhys felt his knee start to bounce restlessly, his thoughts starting to weigh heavy on him.

How fucking pathetic was he that he wouldn't make it one night without hitting up some sort of party?

A knock sounded on the door and Rhys bolted upright, almost running to the door and flinging it open. Luna Sullivan, bandmate and drummer, ran her steely green eyes over him and she nodded, lifting her brows as she said. "Well, you look like a decent meal has done ya good. For a while there, you were starting to look like the fucking dead arisen."

Rhys barked out a laugh, despite himself. "Still subtle like a sledgehammer, Luna."

Luna swept her braid off her shoulder. "That's why everyone loves me. Now, you can wallow in self pity for a few hours but then you're getting out and about and I won't take no for an answer."

The last thing Rhys wanted to do was venture out in public. Andi had managed to keep his accident quiet so no one knew that he'd ended up where he did. She'd also managed to delay the final recording sessions for their album so Rhys could get sorted and back to what he did best.

"Get dressed pretty boy," Luna said as she shoved past him, glancing round the room. "You walking around naked in Cork city will do nothing to keep the media hounds away. Hurry up, I don't have all day."

Rhys rolled his eyes, but still went and did as he was told. Luna Sullivan was a scary SOB when she wanted to be...that girl had bigger balls than most men.

CHAPTER THREE

Shay

SHAY GLEESON DOODLED in her sketch pad in the back room of Rebel Ink, the tattoo shop she managed for her close friend, Cathal Horgan. It might not have been the job she'd pictured for herself, but Shay loved it and she loved the boys of Rebel Ink like family. Considering her own family disowned her because of her career choice, it was a blessing to be surrounded by her little tribe of heathens.

Her father was a solicitor, one who worked for the criminals and drug dealers of the city and Shay had hated it. The extravagant lifestyle her parents were used to was provided by dirty money. When her dad tossed her out when she told him she was going to art school and not getting a law degree to go work for him, Shay had applied for the job at Rebel Ink as a means to pay for rent and food but had gained much more than she'd ever expected.

An only child, Shay had to quickly adapt to being a sister with overprotective brothers, even if she felt sometimes like she was a glorified babysitter.

The memory made her smile as she smudged the outline of her drawing. Her plan had been to manage the shop while working her way to becoming an apprentice. But as Cathal, Isaac, and Darren's reputations grew, the more business they got, and the busier the shop became. And she was too much of a control freak to hand the reigns of the shop over to someone else so she could tattoo.

Besides, the expansion meant that Cathal could hire more artists to work at Rebel Ink, the building next door being renovated so that in another couple of months the shop would be triple the size. Plus Cathal was now dating rockstar Luna Sullivan so Shay basically had to force him onto a plane to spend time with his girlfriend if she was in another country for whatever reason.

The money Cathal made during that time was so bloody good that he couldn't justify not going, even if he worried like the worrier he was.

Cathal's upbringing had been the complete opposite to hers. While she'd attended private school and art classes, Cathal had bounced from foster home to foster home before ending up on the streets as a teenager. Her father had represented the gang leaders who lured kids like Cathal in with the promise of food and safety. Cathal had ended up arrested but instead of prison time, he'd been sent to do community service with the previous owner of Rebel Ink.

That was it for her friend. A few years later he was the owner of Rebel Ink and had a home for the first time in his life and a newfound family. Cathal worked harder than any other person she knew and when he finally let himself be loved, she was glad it was by a woman who didn't back down from a fight and was tough as nails. She called Cathal out when he worked too hard, even though as the drummer for the hottest band around Ireland right now, Luna worked just as hard as Cathal did.

Thankfully today there was no building work going on next door and Cathal was the only artist in the shop so it was fairly quiet. He'd had a few clients to see today, had told Shay to head off but Shay had stayed so he could not be distracted by having to stop to answer the phone or get up when someone walked in.

Shay had suggested locking the door when one of them were there on their own but Cathal had frowned, not wanting to turn a single customer away. That was Cathal all out, a workaholic.

But as Shay continued to doodle in her sketch pad, she kinda wished either Isaac or Darren were around so she at least had someone to else to talk to. But Isaa was on daddy duty today, his six year old Melody, or MJ, was his life and having sole custody of the smart, funny little girl was hard, even though he never complained.

Darren Fitzgerald, or Fitz, was the other resident tattoo artist and it was his turn to take his grandmother and her friends to bingo. They all teased him about it, but Fitz just grinned and said, at this stage, he was in every old biddy's will and set to inherit a fortune. Shay knew that Fitz would do anything for the woman who raised him, after his parents decided a kid was too much hassle.

Shay considered that when you put all of them together, they really shouldn't have worked. However, their little gang of heathens was the only family Shay needed in her life. She would take a bullet for them all.

The door to the shop opened, the little bell signalling someone's arrival. Shay was about to go see who had come in when Luna Sullivan popped her head around the door with a grin on her face.

"Hey Shay," The drummer said in greeting, glancing over her shoulder. "Cathal still working?"

Shay nodded, waving her hand. "Yup, but I'm sure he wouldn't mind being interrupted by you. The rest of us might get annoyed glares but you'll be grand."

Luna laughed, a husky sound. "It's the sex. It's the really good sex."

Shay pulled a face and Luna laughed harder. When you saw them together, Cathal and Luna looked like a rockstar couple but it wasn't only that. They complimented each other so well that they just made sense. .

Luna was crass and outgoing and Cathal was quiet and reserved. Luna loved attention while Cathal was happy to linger on the side-lines.

"Go, before I hear more about my boss's sex life than I ever needed to know."

Luna just grinned, glancing over her shoulder before turning back to Shay. "Hey, you mind keeping an eye on the sour faced idiot outside and making sure he doesn't bolt the minute I'm out of sight?"

Before Shay had a chance to answer, Luna vanished, leaving her to release a sigh and push off the counter, grabbing her sketch pad and pens before heading out to the front of the shop. For a second she thought that whoever Luna had left alone in the reception area of the shop had indeed bolted, but when she got to counter, Shay froze almost dropping her sketch pad.

Rhys Collins, Heartache Melody's keyboard player, and well-known party boy sat hunched in one of the chairs, head bent as he looked at the ground. His leg bounced like he was nervous and his elbows rested on his knees. His dark hair hung in his eyes, and there was a faint line of stubble that the rockstar didn't usually have.

There was something about Rhys today, something vulnerable that squeezed her heart.

This wasn't her first time meeting him, but when he lifted his head to look at her, Shay felt the same lightning bolt to the chest she had felt every time his haunting amber eyes had clashed with hers across the bar, or at a gig.

Rhys looked ...healthier... like he'd added some weight and that just made the sharp angles of his face more arresting. She could understand why fans went crazy when Rhys got on stage with just a tight pair of jeans and a leather jacket.

But Rhys Collins wasn't the kind of guy Shay should be feeling lightning bolts about. His amber eyes looked haunted, even more so than before. He was too handsome, no, handsome wasn't even the word to describe him. Rhys was pretty, with sharp cheekbones and full lips that promised seduction. Even his dark brown hair looked like he'd just gotten out of bed.

Shay knew guys like Rhys - cocky, arrogant, self-assured. A rockstar who was used to women and probably men throwing themselves at him on an hourly basis. Even now, his eyes roamed over her like he was sussing out what his chances were.

Despite the way her body reacted to the rockstar, Shay would keep her feet firmly on the ground and she promised herself she wouldn't end up like her two best friends and fall for the charms of a drop-your-panties gorgeous rockstar.

And hell if that promise didn't taste like ashes on her tongue.

CHAPTER FOUR

Rhys

RHYS FELT the weight of someone's stare on him and it forced his head up, and also forced him out of his thoughts. For the briefest of moments, he had actually considered doing a runner while Luna was getting all lovey-dovey with Cathal. He was minutes from a number of bars and clubs that he could lose himself in the moment he entered.

But he was trying to stick to his word that he would see the ninety days out before he decided to dive back into his old life. Rhys would be damned if he broke his word after a mere couple of hours of freedom.

When Rhys lifted his head, his eyes crashed with green eyes that were dark and haunting. Shay Gleeson was the kind of woman who made men look twice, her slim frame almost too slim but Rhys knew it was down to genetics rather than her feeling like she needed to not eat to stay attractive. She had an array of piercings and ink, and a no-nonsense attitude that made Rhys want to see how long it would take to get her naked.

But that had been before he had royally fucked up.

Rhys knew that Shay ran the shop with an iron fist and like most of the women in his life, she would take no shit from him. Besides, if the Rebel Ink lads were as protective of Shay as the band was of Luna, then they would no doubt chase Rhys off with a hurley if he showed even the slightest interest in Shay...hell, Luna had already warned him off from pursuing Shay.

The woman in question leaned on the counter after setting down what Rhys assumed was a sketch pad and pens, her eyes giving him a once over before she pressed her purple-painted lips closed in a firm line like she was trying to figure out what to say to him.

Running his fingers through his hair, Rhys sat back in the chair. "Luna ask you to keep an eye on me?"

Shay just shrugged her shoulders noncommittedly and Rhys wondered if she was actually gonna speak to him at all or were they gonna sit in awkward silence while waiting for Luna. Rhys watched as Shay pulled herself up on the counter, leaning against the wall for support.

"Family worries," She offered, her tone dark and husky, like whiskey and Rhys leaned forward a little just to hear her a little more. "You should be glad to have people around that care for you even after you've been a dickhead."

Rhys barked out a laugh, shaking his head. "You just gonna take shots at me when you don't know me?"

"I learned long ago that it's best to be upfront about things. I wasn't gonna sit here and pretend that I didn't know what happened and you should appreciate the honesty. Are you saying you haven't been a dickhead?"

Without meaning to, Rhys found himself smiling. "I'm not denying anything. I've been a dickhead. But I've never been a dickhead to you so you don't get to call me on it. You make a habit of judging people on what others have told ya?"

Rhys wanted to be annoyed, hell, he wanted the right to be pissed at Shay for calling him out like she was, at their first proper interaction, and yet, the conversation was making him feel, well, Rhys wasn't sure what he was feeling, but it was invigorating.

To be fair, Shay looked shocked at herself for whatever reason and Rhys wished he could read her thoughts. She reached for her sketchpad, obviously done with her involuntary babysitting of him, and began to focus on her drawing and avoid all eye contact with him.

"What are you drawing?" Rhys asked when the

silence became too much and Shay shifted her gaze to his.

"Nothing much. Just some tattoo ideas."

"So if you manage the shop, when do you get time to tattoo...you're an artist too right?" Rhys asked, genuinely interested, because while he wasn't too keen on the pain of a tattoo, if Shay was tattooing him, Rhys would certainly consider it.

A faint flush darkened Shay's pale skin. "I'm not a tattoo artist...yet. But maybe one day."

"What's holding you back?"

The gorgeous woman glared at him like he had just asked her to strip naked and dance on the counter for him, and while Rhys wasn't exactly opposed to that idea, as someone who was hiding his own talents out of fear, he wanted to know if Shay was a little like him and he longed for someone to understand him like that.

"Hey, I'm sorry. None of my business. I just didn't think Cathal would hold you back even if you are the only one he trusts to manage the shop." When Shay lifted a brow, Rhys reclined in his chair again. "That's what I heard Cathal say."

"Maybe you should mind your own business." Shay snapped, her expression turning stormy, making that tiny spark of anger in his chest force its way to the surface.

With a smug smirk on his face, Rhys indicated to Shay. "Then maybe you should take your own advice, darling, and mind ya business too. You opened the door by calling me a dickhead and talking about things you know shit about."

A muscle in Shay's jaw ticked and she reached under the counter and turned up the music, essentially giving Rhys the middle finger and halting any further opportunities for them to argue. Rhys ducked his head, his hair falling into his eyes once more, and yet, he still watched as Shay bobbed her head in time with the Limp Bizkit song playing.

Well, at least the woman had good taste in music. It almost made up for the attitude.

Eh, pot and kettle, Rhys...pot and kettle.

Rhys snorted at his own thoughts. Yup, he was being a damn hypocrite. His own attitude had been his downfall lately and it was the reason why he relationships with most of his family and friends were blown to hell. Rhys knew he had a lot of bridges to build and pissing off Luna's new boyfriend's best friend wasn't the way to go about it.

The music changed to a Billie Eilish song that he liked to play on the piano. Rhys closed his eyes and used his fingers to play out the keys on his thighs, inhaling and exhaling as he let the music wash over him. Heartache Melody was known for its heavy riffs and drumbeats as well as Declan's killer voice, but sometimes, Rhys liked to take songs that the band wouldn't think of covering and make them his own.

Rhys hadn't meant to start singing along with the

song, but he had got used to just using his voice when he played the piano now and it had lulled him into a false sense of normality. It wasn't until the music stopped suddenly and he heard himself singing which caused him to stumble over the lyrics and he clamped his mouth shut.

His eyes darted open to find that Shay was looking at him with a clearly surprised expression.

"I didn't know that you could sing?"

"I can't. I don't." Rhys heard voices coming from the back and he felt his heart begin to race. "Please, Shay. Forget what you just heard."

Shay frowned, then made to respond when Luna, Cathal and a very happy client came out from the back and Luna came over to where he was sat, nudging his shoulder and glancing at Shay.

"I hope he hasn't caused to much hassle."

Shay held his gaze for a solid minute before she grinned at Luna. "I can handle him. If I can manage to wrangle my three misfits, then I can handle one rockstar."

Cathal, who had just finished saying farewell to his client, chuckled, glancing at Luna. "That's what I thought too. I was dead wrong."

Rhys glanced at Luna, saw his friend grin, her eyes all shiny and loved up as she bounced to her feet and went to kiss Cathal on the cheek. "But you know I like the way you handle me."

Rhys groaned at the innuendo, as Cathal just shook his head. "You ready to go eat?"

Oh for fuck sake. There was no way Rhys wanted to play third wheel with Luna and Cathal. He got to his feet, readying his excuses when Cathal turned to Shay. "Come on, Shay. I'm paying."

Nobody seemed to notice that Shay was looking at him and Rhys kept his expression guarded as the woman who knew his secret slipping off the counter and grinned. "I'll never refuse a free meal. Let's go, I'm starving."

Shay ducked into the back and Luna angled her head to look at him. "Rhys? You'll come eat with us?"

Maybe it was the way Luna said it, but she fully expected him to refuse and cause a scene. But Rhys was hungry so he just nodded, waiting until Shay had come out with a leather jacket on to grin and reply. "I could eat. Since Cathal is paying, I could eat."

CHAPTER FIVE

Shay

SHAY HAD BEEN TAKEN ABACK when Cathal had suggested they go out for food, even more so when Rhys had agreed to go with them. He had been quiet on the walk over to the restaurant, even more so after they had ordered drinks and the rockstar had ordered a Coke. Luna had looked pleased and had ordered one herself, with her and Cathal having already ordered a beer.

Luna and Cathal were chatting now about something Oli Scott was planning. Oli was an even bigger rockstar than Luna and her band, but he and Cathal had fallen into a friendship that surprised even Luna, but Shay was happy that Cathal was making friends outside of the shop.

It was like Cathal was getting his teen and early twenty years back now that he'd found Luna.

Shay kept trying to catch Rhys' eye, feeling the need to assure him that she wasn't going to spill his secrets to anyone. When Shay had heard the keyboardist start to sing, she had been so utterly shocked that she had wanted to make sure she wasn't imagining what she was hearing.

That had startled Rhys and he had fumbled lyrics, his eyes opening with a look that could only be described as terror. Shay had heard Luna and Jameson repeatedly tease Rhys for his lack of singing ability, and Shay had unfortunately heard the croak that Luna called her singing voice.

But unlike Luna's screeching, Rhys had a subtle, almost pureness to its tone. He didn't have that harsh gruff tone that Declan Walsh was renowned for, nor was it like Jameson's emotionally charged voice. No there was something entirely different about Rhys' singing voice and Shay was curious to find out more.

Cathal dragged her into his and Luna's conversation, the pair not noticing how quiet Rhys was being. The man that Shay wanted to strangle one minute and kiss the next was looking out of the window, stirring his Coke around so that the ice clinked against the glass. Anyone who looked at him could see that he looked lost.

As if he sensed her watching him, Rhys turned his head to look at her and Shay hated that Rhys affected her with just one look. His lips parted as if he was going to remark, then the waitress arrived with their food, grinning at Rhys, but to her surprise, and Luna's too from the look in the drummer's face, Rhys didn't so much as glance in the woman's direction as she set down his pasta dish.

The sheer look of disappointment on the woman's face made Shay want to laugh. When Shay and Luna's eyes met, Luna just shrugged, a flash of worry crossing her face as she pushed her plate of chips toward Rhys, who shook his head.

"I'm grand, Luna."

Rhys shoved a forkful of his pasta into his mouth, making a show of chewing and swallowing before he quirked a brow, as if to challenge Luna to say something. Luna's phone pinged and she checked it, typing out a message, giving the game away when she looked at Rhys, who just happened to be staring at her.

"You can report back to Andi, or Declan, or whoever is checking on me that I haven't had a drink, I didn't chat up the waitress or head to the bathrooms for a quick fuck. You can tell them I'm eating food and not causing any trouble. You can also tell them that the micromanaging and babysitting is getting old fast and more likely to drive me to have a drink."

Cathal bristled at the harshness in Rhys' tone, especially since it was directed at Luna, but Shay kicked him under the table, because apart from the tone, Rhys hadn't really said anything that wasn't the truth.

The rest of the meal was eaten in relative silence, reminding Shay of dinners that she had had when she still lived at home, forced to attend formal family dinners each evening where conversation was the bare minimum. It had been torture.

When they had all finished eating, Cathal called for the bill and Rhys surged to his feet, telling Luna he would wait outside while they paid. Luna made to follow after him but Rhys tossed her a dark look that had Luna stopping in her tracks. Rhys stalked out into the night air, but stayed in view as he went and leaned on the wall outside, his arms folded across his chest and his eyes closed.

"Andi said he was still so angry, but I didn't realize how much he was."

Luna's words were spoken so softly, Shay almost missed them. "Maybe he just needs to feel like he's in control. I know if I felt everyone was watching me as if they were waiting for me to fuck up, I'd be pissed. When I broke my foot, the boys were so suffocating I threatened to castrate the lot of them."

Luna laughed, the tension easing from her face. "Oh, I know. They were all like that when I was mugged. I'll tell Andi that...it might help."

Shay reached out and gave her arm a squeeze, then let the couple alone as she went outside to where Rhys was standing. "Luna's worried about you."

Huffing out what Shay could only describe as a frustrated breath, Rhys clenched his fists, then flatted his palms. "I know. I know, okay. Everyone's worried Rhys is gonna screw up and fuck over the band. I know I brought it on myself but Jesus Christ, I need a minute. I just need a fucking minute."

There was a staggering amount of pain weaved into Rhys' words that Shay could totally understand. He had made some mistakes, sure, and yet, with everyone watching him, how was Rhys supposed to carry on when everyone was already setting him up for failure?

Shay leaned against the wall beside Rhys and glanced over. "Maybe you should just tell them how you are feeling and what you need. It might not help, but it couldn't hurt."

"You make it sound so easy," Rhys replied, running those talented fingers through his hair. "But every time I open my mouth I end up saying the wrong thing. So, what's the point?"

Shay didn't know what to say in response, and when she didn't say anything to his question, Rhys sighed. "Sorry. Not really sure why I just offloaded to you."

Nudging Rhys with her shoulder, Shay grinned. "Comes with the territory. When you work front of shop, people come in with tattoo ideas and they tell you their life story. Cathal once referred to getting a tattoo as a form of therapy session, so maybe that's it. Plus, I'm on the outside looking in. I'm not here to judge you."

A look of surprise flashed across Rhys' features before he pulled his gaze away. He rubbed his palms on his jeans and inhaled, like he was readying to say something, but Luna and Cathal strode out of the restaurant and Rhys clamped his lips shut.

"Right, Rhys, you can come back to Cathal's with us and watch a movie or something. Shay, you too!"

Shay was already shaking her head when Rhys interjected. "Luna, I'm gonna head home."

"But it's still early!"

Lifting her gaze to Cathal, Shay tried to tell him with just a look that Luna needed to dial it back, and Cathal took notice, slipping his hand into Luna's. "Rhys probably just wants to get some sleep, Luna."

Rhys looked like he could have kissed Cathal as Luna pouted, obviously not happy that her boyfriend was siding with the man she was trying to look after. Cathal looked at Shay, all wide-eyed as if he didn't know what to do now, and if it wasn't for the tension, Shay might have even laughed.

"Cathal's right, Luna," Rhys began, pushing off the wall. "I just wanna go home and crash in my own bed. Thanks for dinner."

Rhys reached out and pulled Luna in for a hug, then fist-bumped Cathal, before turning to her. Shay wanted to ignore the galloping of her heart, the way her body seemed to come alive as Rhys smiled at her, those amber eyes of his so enticing. "See ya around, Shay."

Shay frowned as she watched Rhys stride away, and heard Luna mutter about finding him in some bar in the morning. But Rhys walked straight to the taxi rank and jumped into the back, leaving them standing there in the cold night air.

"I should call Declan," Luna said as she pulled out her phone, and Shay felt irritated on Rhys' behalf as she listened to Luan tell Declan that Rhys had supposedly gone home in a taxi.

"Maybe they should give him the benefit of the doubt." Shay heard herself mutter, not meaning to say the words out loud.

"Let it go, Shay," Cathal warned her. "It's not for us to interfere."

Shay wanted to protest, to say something, however, the look on Cathal's face was enough for her to remain quiet. And Cathal was right...Rhys Collins wasn't her responsibility. It would probably be best if they stayed away from one another.

CHAPTER SIX

Rhys

RHYS HAD DONE EXACTLY what he had said he was going to do last night. He'd gotten into the taxi and gone straight home, throwing himself on the bed, and had fallen into a deep sleep without even trying. He still woke feeling exhausted this morning, laying in bed with no clue what he was gonna do for the day.

His usual routine, pre the window incident, had been to walk at like noon after getting in maybe at four in the morning, rehearse with the band or record, then hit up any party that might be happening if the band had no gig. But since Rhys was trying to stay away from all that crap, and it was just after nine, the day seemed to him like it was gonna drag.

When he was in the retreat, getting up early hadn't really bothered him because their day was filled with things to do, and he didn't have time to sit and fester. And yet here he was, not even twenty-four hours home and he was bored and unsure what to do with himself.

What he really wanted was to sit down in front of his piano and play, but his piano was at Declan's studio, and going there might mean running into Declan or one of his bandmates. Rhys had a few keyboards here at home, but he had gotten used to playing the piano every day and now it felt like part of the routine he needed to keep in order to clear his head.

After staring at the ceiling for a good hour, Rhys heaved himself out of bed and went and had a shower, throwing on jeans and a t-shirt, before going to make some breakfast. He was a terrible cook...a skill he never thought a rockstar needed, and he had been spoilt with his mam's cooking and then, grabbing fast food when he was dying with a hangover. This meant his choices were slim this morning.

After a breakfast of dry cereal and some toast, Rhys brushed his teeth and grabbed a hoody before he spied his car keys hanging up. It had been months since he'd been in any condition to drive it, and Rhys wasn't sure if the car had any petrol in it.

He was pleasantly surprised to see not only did he have a full tank of petrol, but it was spotlessly clean. Someone must have cleaned out all the rubbish and made sure it was running before he got home from the retreat. Rhys would have shot off a text to the band's group chat, however, he was still minus a phone.

Declan probably had it...

That was Declan all-out – making Rhys come to him and ask for the phone back so Rhys would have no choice but to talk to him. Rhys knew it was probably childish of him to not want to have Declan in his face right now...where Declan would be all up on his high horse and lay down the law to him about his behaviour and his future with the band.

But Rhys knew that Declan was a massive trigger for him. That's what they had called it. it wasn't exactly his relationship with Andi that set Rhys off, but Declan himself. When the therapist had told him that, Rhys had laughed, shaking his head, clearly disagreeing with the woman who was way smarter than he was.

"Just think on it for a moment, Rhys." Dr. Shannon asked him, making him shift a little in his seat. "When you were young and struggling with your dyslexia, Declan was there to help keep the bullies away. You looked up to him and he was your best friend first. But you've always wondered if Declan stayed your friend because he was in love with your sister."

Was that really what was eating Rhys? He hadn't been sure at all during his thirty day holiday but when he had walked out the main door and seen that it was only Andi waiting for him, Rhys had been relieved. So maybe the doctor wasn't talking all shite, like Rhys had told her.

"You'll never be able to move on and be exactly who you are supposed to be if you do not explain to those around you how you feel. The healing comes from speaking the truth to those who love you."

Rhys parked the car in a spot outside Declan's and rested his head on the steering wheel for a minute. The problem was he didn't know where to start. Any conversations Rhys had to have wouldn't be easy ones, and he wasn't good at apologizing for shit he'd done. His actions had put the band at risk, delayed their album release which cost a hell of a lot of money, and jeopardized the livelihoods of the entire band.

It also messed with his sister's reputation, and even being a complete idiot, Rhys knew Andi was good for the band...more than good. His sister was this power-house PR mogul, who knew music and understood what it took to get them attention. While he wasn't sure how he felt about Andi and Declan together, Rhys was actually grateful that Andi was part of the band's success.

Now, if only he could find the right words to tell her.

Getting out of the car, Rhys locked it, then opened the main door. There were stairs to the right that led up to Declan's loft apartment, where his sister currently lived. Straight ahead of him was the door to the studio, where the band rehearsed, where they hung out, and where they recorded a lot of their songs. Rhys considered heading up the stairs and trying to make amends, and yet, the nausea in the pit of his stomach made him key in the code on the studio door and head inside.

Thankfully, the space was empty, the hang out area was very still and quiet compared to how it usually was. Rhys headed straight back to the recording areas, checking first to make sure no one was hiding out in one of the spaces, and considering Oli Scott liked to show up whenever he liked recently, finding someone in one of the rooms wouldn't have shocked him.

It was blissfully quiet, thankfully as Rhys went into the wide open room where he had recorded a lot of the piano for the album. Himself and Declan had picked it out, Declan waving him off when Rhys offered to pay for the piano by himself. Rhys had fallen in love with it the moment he had laid eyes on it in the shop.

It felt like ages since he had sat down and played it. The last time was probably when Luna and Cathal had brought MJ, the little girl of one of the tattoo artists, and he had sat with her and helped her play a little. It had been the most fun he'd had in a long time.

Closing the door behind him, then he slipped off his hoodie, tossing it aside, Rhys sat down in front of the piano and traced his fingers along the ivory keys. A sense of peace washed over him, and he exhaled, closing his eyes, letting the silence linger for a fraction of a heartbeat and then his fingers glided over the keys.

The first bars of Harry Styles *As It Was* rang out in the room before he switched it up and started Ed Sheeran's *Bad Habits*. He had never liked learning to play the classical music his tutors had forced him to learn, preferring to learn how to play other songs like Meatloaf's *I would do anything for love* or anything current.

Andi had always loved to play anything. Their music teachers had adored his sister, who had been the more talented of the Collin's siblings by all accounts and Rhys would always be second where Andi was concerned.

Rhys could feel that sliver of anger inside his chest as he switched songs and started The Fray's *Be Still*, hoping the song would alleviate his errant thoughts and stop his destructive train of thought. He always did this, made himself the runner-up where Andi was concerned. He never felt he was good enough, never felt like he was talented enough.

His struggle with education due to his dyslexia had always felt like it crippled him, but somehow, reading music and understanding music had never been hard for him. It saved him really. Even now when nothing in his life felt certain, music had saved Rhys.

The song finished and as Rhys considered what song he would play next, a polite cough alerted him that he wasn't alone anymore. Slowly opening his eyes,

Rhys angled his face toward his sister, who lingered in the doorway with a grin on her face. Andi stepped into the room, making to come towards him but then she stopped, a hesitation that hurt Rhys more than he cared to admit.

He had done this to them...he had fractured their bond.

"Jesus," Andi said, her grin still as wide despite her hesitation. "I had forgotten how much I loved to sit and watch you play."

CHAPTER SEVEN

Rhys

RHYS WASN'T sure he had the right response for what Andi had just said, so he made to rise off the piano stool. Andi frowned, taking a step toward him, a hesitant step that seemed to rankle Rhys, as if he were a cornered animal to be approached with extreme caution.

But he really was, wasn't he?

"I didn't mean to interrupt, Rhys. I just saw you were down here and wanted to ... see how you were. I wasn't going to intrude, but I couldn't not listen to you play."

His sister, the take no prisoners, balls-of-steel sister, who never soft-soaped anything in her life, was being overtly polite with him and it felt…strained. But Rhys knew that his conflicted feelings and his downright stupid actions were responsible for this overtly reserved Andi.

"You haven't looked so content in a long time. It was beautiful."

Rhys snorted, embarrassed by her words, and yet, he felt like he couldn't trust them. "Cut the bullshit, Andi. We both know that you're the better pianist."

Andi looked surprised at his remark, even more so because Rhys hadn't been able to mask the resentment in his tone.

"Rhys," She replied, walking around to lean on the piano. "That was never true. Do you not remember Mrs. Canning? She said time and time again that if the classical music didn't bore you so much you could have played Carnegie Hall. But she said that your mind was so busy that the usual piano pieces bored you."

Rhys hadn't thought of his and Andi's first piano teacher in a long time, however, he remembered the conversation with his parents about something Mrs. Canning had said after one lesson.

Rhys slumped down in his chair, fully convinced that he was in trouble with his parents. He hadn't meant to give Mrs. Canning cheek, but she kept trying to make him play boring old classical music piano pieces and wasn't at all pleased when Rhys tried to incorporate rock songs into the ancient material.

"You're not in trouble, Rhys." His dad said as he

lowered himself into the seat beside Rhys, nudging his shoulder and grinning.

"I saw Mrs. Canning talking to ya. I thought she was giving out."

Rhys ducked his head, strands of his hair falling into his eyes. His mam lifted his head by placing her hand under his chin, forcing Rhys to look into his mother's eyes.

"We know it's been hard at school since you found out you had dyslexia, baby. But we never cared about grades once you put in the effort. You were born to play piano. It's your gift and Mrs. Canning just wants to make sure that the gift you have can take you to places beyond Ireland. She wants to make sure that she can give you the tools to do that."

"But the classical stuff bores me...I'm not like Andi. She's better than me at everything."

"Oh Rhys," His mam sighed, a sheen of wetness in her eyes. "You and your sister are two different people. Andi likes classical and you don't. That's perfectly fine. But you need to learn the pieces so you can do more. And Mrs. Canning will help you. You just need to concentrate and let her teach you."

Rhys hadn't thought much on it over the years, even if he had done as his parents asked him, perfecting the pieces until one day when Mrs. Canning brought him a book of the best rock piano songs and then Rhys truly knew he could excel.

Being dyslexic had been hard in school. But his

parents never made him feel any different or tried to force his to be good at it. Rhys sometimes had trouble reading things, the words jumbled in his head. He got frustrated about it because he didn't want to be labelled as the dumb kid in class.

He didn't have many other friends, content to hang out with Andi, but when they went to secondary school and his friend from music school Declan, attended the same school, life had gotten so much easier for him.

Sliding over to give Andi room to sit, Rhys tinkled with the keys as Andi came and sat down beside him. Rhys took stock of her out of the corner of his eye, and Andi looked tired, drained even.

"I haven't thought of Mrs. Canning in years," Rhys admitted, lifting his eyes to look directly at Andi. "She's a major reason why I get to play this way."

Andi grinned, nudging him with her shoulder. "You were always her favourite. She would always brag to other mothers that one day, Rhys Collins would be a rockstar."

"And I might have thrown that away." Rhys admitted with a sigh. "Declan might kick me out of the band. Hell, he'd probably prefer to have you in the band now that you two...yano?"

Andi narrowed her gaze. "That's not going to happen, Rhys. You and Declan will sort it out. And I would never want to take your place. Do you really think I would do that?"

Her words were soft but they rang with hurt and pain. Rhys ran a hand through his hair. "No." He assured Andi, the relief on her face evident. "I know you wouldn't. I'm just not sure how I can get back in Declan's good graces. Every conversation we have lately ends in some sort of verbal fight."

Andi was quiet for a time, as Rhys played a few bars from Metallica's *Nothing Else Matters*, letting Andi make sense of what she needed to. Rhys knew it probably wasn't fair, him having this conversation about Andi's boyfriend and that was part of the problem he had.

For the longest time, Rhys had only had Andi as a friend and confidant. Then he had Declan. Now the two people he loved the most had each other...and it still annoyed Rhys why he was so confused about what that meant now...he felt like he'd been cut out of their lives.

"Why did you do it, Rhys?" Andi asked him softly, her own hand resting on the piano keys. "I understand that you like to party. I understand all the one night hook-ups. But drugs? Why would you do that?"

"You'll never be able to move on and be exactly who you are supposed to be if you do not explain to those around you how you feel. The healing comes from speaking the truth to those who love you."

Dr. Shannon's words popped into his head and although Rhys would have ignored Andi's question, if he wanted to get back to where he wanted to be, if he wanted to start to live the life he wanted, then he needed to start being honest with everyone around him and maybe starting with Andi was the way to go.

"I know you don't believe me, but that night was the first and last night. I swear to ya." Rhys began, setting his hands in his lap before continuing. "I was overthinking...a lot. And I was angry at you, at Dec, hell even at Jameson for being so nauseatingly happy. It made me feel like a bastard and I just wanted to not think, even for a couple of hours. That's why I did the cocaine. I just wanted to stop hating myself for a minute."

It felt awkward, admitting that to Andi, but he felt like it was the start of unburdening himself, and he heard Andi sniffle, Rhys reached out and took his sisters hand and gave it a squeeze.

"You have to promise you'll never do that again." Andi said finally, a fierceness in her tone. "If you feel like that again, you come to me. I am never too busy for you, Rhys. Never."

Rhys cleared his throat to try and get rid of the emotion that suddenly seemed to make his throat feel tight. "Okay, Andi. And I promise. I know I shouldn't have done it in the first place."

Andi threw her arms around him, engulfing him in a hug, and Rhys could do nothing wrap his arms around her in return. They stayed like that for a while, until Andi let him go. She swiped the tears from her eyes, then offered him a smile.

"Why don't you come up stairs? We can talk and have some dinner."

While he was glad that he had taken a step forward with Andi, Rhys wasn't ready to take that step with Declan and his face must have shown it because Andi frowned, muttering that they were both as bad as one another.

"I think I'm just gonna sit and play for a bit, if that's okay? But maybe we can get lunch or dinner during the week? Just us...like old times."

It was an olive branch, but not much of one and Rhys knew that Andi would feel conflicted that the two men in her life couldn't be in the same room as one another at the moment. But his sister just smiled and replied. "I'd like that, Rhys. Do you mind if I sit and listen to you while you play? To clear my own head?"

Rhys didn't answer Andi, just started to play one of her favourite songs, and she leaned her head against him as he played and for a moment, Rhys felt like everything was right in the world again.

CHAPTER EIGHT

Shay

SHAY WAS BORED out of her fucking mind.

She sat across the table from her date, Barry, a handsome client of Isaac's who had asked her out for dinner, and who had the personality of a dishcloth. Barry worked in investments, made his money dealing with wealthy clients who took his advice on how to invest in stocks and bonds and lots of stuff that Shay had absolutely no interest in.

But Barry had been rabbiting on for nearly an hour about his summer house and lad's trips to pompous rich people places, and Shay had almost fallen asleep with her eyes open. Even now, her chin was resting on her fist as she leaned on the table, her eyes open but her mind had already wandered as she looked at the fire that was burning from a stove and casting shadows in the darkened restaurant, an idea for a new tattoo design popping into her mind and she wanted to be done with this date so she could go home and sketch the idea out.

Shay hadn't even wanted to go on the date, but Isaac had convinced her that Barry was a good guy and Shay should give him a chance, to which Shay had asked if she could fix Isaac up with one of her old college friends. Isaac had rolled his eyes, telling Shay that he only had time for one girl in his life and dating wasn't in the cards for him.

She'd agreed to the date just to see the distressed look in Issacs's eyes vanish.

They had just finished eating. Barry was still drinking a glass of expensive wine and that should have been a clear indication that Barry and her were just two different kinds of people, because she was drinking a pint. The restaurant was far posher that Shay liked to dine in, but she had come here a few times with her parents, when she was younger.

"Shay"

Oh shit, Barry had obviously asked her something and she had totally blanked him.

"I'm sorry," she offered with a terse smile. "What did you say?"

Barry was obviously used to women who listened as he spoke and hung on his every word because he gave her a look of distain that almost made Shay laugh out loud. Barry held up his hand and clicked his fingers, summoning the waitress for the bill, an action that annoyed Shay as she gathered her jacket and bag, getting out her purse to pay her share, annoyed at herself that it would eat up most of her savings for the month.

Barry slid the waitress a black sleek credit card, brushing off her attempts to pay. He walked her out the door, his hand on the small of her back, turning to her when they stepped away from the door, and Shay hoped he wasn't about to ask for a second date.

"Shay."

A sense of dread crept along her spine as Shay turned to see her father standing on the footpath looking at her. He had aged since the last time she saw him, with grey strands now intertwined with his black hair. His eyes were still as sharp as ever and they ran over her in assessment before coming back up to hold her gaze.

"Dad."

That was the only greeting Shay had in her to offer him because she didn't have any other platitudes to offer him. she wasn't happy to see him. She didn't want to tell him he looked well, and from the rounded belly, well tailored suit and gold cuff links, her dad was still rich as fuck.

"Still forsaking your art degree to work at the convict's tattoo studio?"

"Still making money by helping Cork's criminal underworld stay out of prison?" Shay tossed back, barely glancing over her shoulder as Barry make a swift and cowardly exit, no doubt having realized who her father was.

Her dad's face remained impassive, but Shay saw a muscle twitch in his face, the only indication that Shay was pushing his buttons as much as he was pushing hers.

Glancing at his watch, Seamus Gleeson, huffed out an exaggerated breath, then completely ignored his only child and strode into the restaurant, where Shay watched as he shook hands with a well known gang boss, then made their way to the more exclusive, elite back rooms for privacy.

Shat wanted to storm into the restaurant and start shouting the odds at her dad, the hurt and anger she felt towards him, and her mother who supported her husband and not her child, seeping into her bloodstream until her entire body was shaking.

"Shay?"

Shay jerked as she felt a hand graze her arm, whirling around to see a very sweaty Rhys Collins looking at her with concern in his eyes.

"Jayus, you look like you're about to cut a bitch."

Rhys flashed her a very sexy half grin that made Shay bark out a laugh and move way from the restaurant and her father. Rhys fell into step beside her, and Shay leaned on the railing by the river and looked at Rhys.

He was dressed in shorts that came down to his

knees, a hoody that was too big for him but Shay suspected it might have fit him at some stage, the sleeves rolled up. His face was slick with sweat and his face was as striking as it always had been, but he seemed more relaxed since the last time she saw him.

He tapped the side of his earphone, then took it out of his ear and repeated the action with the other, stashing them in the pocket of his hoody before he spoke. "Not gonna lie and pretend I didn't see the interaction with your ole man. Or the fact that the frat boy did a runner."

"It's nothing." Shay replied, the lie coming out with a little more harshness than she intended. Rhys held up his hands in a show of peace.

"Hey, I'm just checking to make sure you're okay. Let me walk ya home."

A flush crept over her skin at the innocent words, but if her face had gotten red, Rhys didn't seem to notice as they headed off toward Shay's tiny bedsit on the other side of the city, near to the tattoo shop. Neither of them spoke for the longest time, and Shay wondered why Rhys was out late running the streets in the dark, and when she asked him, the rockstar didn't seem reluctant to answer him.

"I got used to working out while I was ... away. Running by day means more chance of getting recognised, than if I run at night. Plus then I'm so fucking wrecked that all I want to do is go to bed. Less chance of me overthinking shit and wanting to go party."

Shay blinked at the brutal honesty and her face must have shown her surprise because Rhys chuckled, a warm, gravelly sound that made Shay want to hear it again. If she wasn't careful, she'd embarrass herself in front of the man she had a foolish crush on.

She wasn't about to be another notch on the Rhys Collins bedpost...as tantalising as it sounded, or how much her body wanted her to indulge on her little fantasy.

"I get it," Shay found herself saying. "Luna tells us all the time how she gets stopped on a run to sign autographs. I mean, if someone snaps her at the shop, we have fans turning up just to peer though the window."

Rhys grinned over at her. "Jamie has that problem when he works a shift at Rebel Books. It used to bother him so much he'd text me to come over and pose in the corner like I was auditioning for the Insta page, Hot Dudes Reading."

Shay laughed, shaking her head. "I bet you loved the attention."

Rhys ducked his head, as if embarrassed. "I did, once. Now it's just a part of the job. It's like I'm two different people – the Rhys Collins who is the ultimate showman on stage and the Rhys who is just tired of it all. Hell, sometimes, I don't even like myself."

Shay reached out and grabbed Rhys elbow. "Hey, you're not so bad. And I know that the onstage persona can be different. I was worried for Sinéad when she started dating Jameson. And Cathal. But

Jameson and Luna are awesome people. You must be too if they let you hang with them."

Amber eyes ablaze in the dark of the night, Shay watched as Rhys swallowed then expertly changed the subject, asking Shay if she had any new designs she was working on. She told Rhys about the flames and the shadows and her ideas, and he listened intently, far more than she expected.

Shay found herself laughing and smiling as Rhys walked her home, then waited until she was inside before he popped in his headphones and took off running, and Shay watched him until his shadow disappeared.

Rhys Collins was a distraction she didn't need in her life, but her curiosity might just be her downfall.

CHAPTER NINE

Shay

SHAY WAS sill thinking about the enigma that was Rhys Collins on Sunday when they were trying to decide on a colour scheme for the shop when it reopened. The shop was closed for the day and next week, much to Cathal's stress, the shop would close for two weeks while they knocked out the existing wall and created the bigger space that Cathal had been planning for the last couple of years.

Today, her friend and boss was stressed out that the shop would be closed and would remain closed if there were any delays in the building work. He also couldn't stay in his apartment while the renovations were going on, but had declined Shay's offer of her couch in favour of crashing at Luna's brother's new place that he shared with his partner, Danish soccer sensation Emil Anderson.

Isaac and Darren had taken the piss out of Cathal, telling him he was fast becoming celebrity tattoo artist and soon enough, some TV producer would come knocking about a reality show because his of his girlfriend and new best friend, Oli Scott.

The very idea had made Cathal turn a very ghostly pale ass white which made the boys laugh even harder.

So that was why Shay was here, talking Cathal off the ledge while Luna was spending the day with Luke and the boys were told to stay away, for Cathal's sanity, and Darren and Isaac's protection. Considering they had decided to gut the entire ground floor, including the old shop and the new shop, it was a big project but would be so freakin cool once it was all done.

And while Cathal was looking at paint samples and going over the final plans for the millionth time, Shay sat on one of the storage boxes, staring out the window as he thoughts drifted back to Rhys.

Two days had passed since he walked her home and two days Shay had been running back over their conversation in her head. Shay had always been a fan of Heartache Melody's music, way back when they played gigs to like fifty people. Even in her teens, the amber eyed Rhys had drawn her attention, but never in her wildest dreams would she have imagined that she would be walking and talking with him.

She also spent a lot of time over the last forty-eight hours chastising herself for being all dreamy-eyed where Rhys was concerned. She was a strong independent woman who did not fawn over ridiculously pretty rockstars with sinful lips and heavenly eyes. And Rhys wasn't even her type! She tended to stay away from pretty boys, and when she did date tended to go for rough and ready looking guys.

But there was something about Rhys that Shay couldn't stop thinking about.

"Hello, Shay? You awake?"

Shay blinked her eyes and looked up to see her best friend, Sinéad Kelleher looking at her with an amused expression, carrying a tray of coffee in her hands. Sinéad had recently moved back to Ireland, having moved to Spain to get away from her obsessive stepbrother who had kidnapped her and killed a young girl with his car. The girl, Layla, had been dating Jameson Kent at the time and Sinéad and Jameson had fallen for each other, though getting them to a good place where they were happy hadn't been easy.

"She's been like that all day," griped Cathal as he took the coffee Sinéad held out for him. "I dunno what's gotten into her."

Sinéad slid her gaze to Shay, who took her own coffee and turned away, rolling her eyes as she did. "I've been zoning out because you've been bitching and moaning all afternoon. My brain hurts listening to you question all the decisions you've already made!"

Cathal gave her a one finger salute and Sinéad burst out laughing, shaking her head as she asked. "What are you trying to decide on?"

"Paint colour." Both Shay and Cathal replied in unison, making Sinéad roll her eyes. "You're both artists. This should be an easy thing to sort out."

Cathal shrugged, leaning against one of the walls. "I decided to go for black and grey with the furniture and the workstations. But I can't stand the thought of boring white walls...or fucking beige."

Shay joined Sinéad in her laughter as Cathal shuddered at the thought of it. They sipped their coffee and chatted for a bit before Cathal's phone rang and he got this stupid ass grin on his face. He glanced over at her and Sinéad.

"Go and sweet talk your girlfriend," Shay ordered him, waving him out. "Maybe she can talk some sense into you."

Sinéad pulled over another storage box and plonked down beside Shay, taking a drink of coffee before Shay asked her where Jameson was.

"Oh he's working a shift for Niamh across the road," Sinéad said with a smile that was full of love and contentment. "I said I'd pop over with coffees and see how you were after bumping into your dad."

Sinéad knew all about Shay's strained relationship with her parents, and Shay had texted Sinéad when she had gotten home. But for some reason, Shay hadn't shared with her oldest friend that Rhys had walked her home. To be honest, Shay wasn't sure why she had kept that part to herself, but she had.

"Earth to Shay. I've lost you again. What are you thinking about that keeps making you day dream?"

Shay tried to school her features, but Sinéad knew all her tells.

"Or is it a who...oh my god, Shay your face...you have to spill now!"

Shay sent down her coffee and rested her chin in her hands. "You're not gonna stop until I tell you, are you?"

"Would you prefer if I ask Cathal if anyone has been hanging around the shop lately that might be sexy enough to snare your attention?"

"For fuck sake, Sinéad...don't bloody do that. It's nothing really and if I tell you, you can't think it means anything or make a big deal about it. Promise me or I'm not gonna tell ya."

Sinéad held out her pinky finger, forcing Shay to loop her own against it, just like when they were kids. Then Shay told Sinéad about after the cold interaction with her dad, bumping into Rhys, and then how he walked her home. She didn't tell her what was shared between them, because that conversation had been private and Shay wasn't gonna betray a confidence.

Her friend listened intently and studied Shay like she was trying to get inside her head, which considering that was part of Sinéad's actual qualification, it was quite easy.

"Don't you dare judge me, Sinéad Kelleher."

Sinéad cast her an evil glare. "Would I ever or have I ever done that?"

Shay offered a smile in way of an apology, then sighed. "It's just Rhys being a nice guy and making sure I got home after he witnessed the thing with my dad. But..."

"But you can't get him out of your head?" Sinéad ventured, a smile of her own curving her lips.

"That's insane, right? I'm losing my goddamn mind, right?"

"Listen," Sinéad started with a grin. "I can't say anything considering the fact that even after my first interaction with Jameson, I couldn't get the idiot out of my head. And Rhys is very, very pretty to look at, if you like that sort of thing. But Shay..."

Her friend trailed off, glancing over her shoulder to make sure they were still alone before she continued. "I won't interfere. If you want to explore your attraction to Rhys, go for it. Let me just say this as someone who fell for a man who was emotionally shattered. Be careful with your heart because Rhys could break it without meaning to. It's not easy being with someone who has emotional baggage."

Shay was about to respond that she wasn't sure her and Rhys could be viewed in the same light as Sinéad and Jameson, when Cathal strode back in and told them that Luna said they needed to make a fucking decision and be done with it.

Sinéad looked around the building, then shrugged. "You guys are the best artists I know. You should all take a wall and design something arty for it. Show off your skills and decorate the walls. No boring beige required."

Cathal stared at Sinéad like he couldn't believe what she was saying and then he smacked himself quite hard on the forehead. "We are fucking idiots and Sinéad is a genius. That makes totally bloody sense."

With that settled, Cathal texted Darren and Isaac to get working on something for their wall, Shay already starting to come up with ideas for her wall, Cathal giving her a look when she asked if she could be involved, but since she wasn't exactly a tattoo artist, she wanted to be certain.

"So, what are you planning on doing?" Sinéad asked her, but Shay just stared at the blank wall and itched to paint something in the richest amber she could find.

CHAPTER TEN

Rhys

"LET me get you another plate, Rhys."

His mam had been trying to overfeed him all afternoon, and Rhys felt as if he was about to burst out of his jeans if his mam forced him to eat one more bite. When he had called yesterday to ask if it was okay if he called over, his mam had been so happy she'd gone out and bought all of his favourite foods.

His parents had always been free spirits, having met at a festival way back when, and they had raised their kids to be who they wanted to be. They were never strict, really, just let them make their own mistakes and helped them to accept the consequences.

But even Rhys could see that his latest actions had

taken a toll on them, his dad's hair a little greyer and his mam, well, she just looked so tired. And even though Rhys was stuffed to the gills, he smiled and replied. "I'm grand, Ma. But I'll take any leftovers. I'll have food for days."

That had appeased his mam a little and she busied herself in getting the mountain of food together for him. His dad came out of the kitchen and handed him a beer, surprise in his eyes when Rhys declined and rose to put the alcohol back in the fridge, taking out a bottle of Coke instead.

Despite the fact that he had been dreading facing them, the afternoon had been pleasant enough and while his mam sorted dinner, Rhys had sat with his dad and watch the hurling, something he hadn't done in the longest time, not since music took over his life.

Rhys had been surprised when Andi hadn't turned up to dinner, knowing his sister tried to have Sunday dinner with their parents as much as possible when she was home. It made him wonder if Andi had stayed away on purpose, to give Rhys time alone with his parents.

Or maybe they were all just trying to keep him and Declan as far apart as possible.

Rhys got up from the table and went into the kitchen, filing the sink with warm water to wash the ware. His mam glanced at him, telling him she would do it, but Rhys was already shaking his head.

"Nah, let me do it. Least I can do, ma, when you

cooked. Besides, I need to work off the food or the fans will be disappointed when I take off my shirt on stage."

His ma narrowed her gaze. "You know you're handsome, Rhys. And it's good to see you looking healthy. Helps me sleep better at night."

Rhys tossed the tea towel over his shoulder and opened his arms, letting his mam wrap her arms around his waist and she embraced him so tightly, it was as if she was afraid to let him go. He didn't want his parents to worry about him, not in the slightest, and he knew that they only knew a sliver of the stupid shit he'd done over the last few months. He understood he had been a terrible son, and a pretty deplorable human being recently.

"Andi said that you two were going for lunch or something next week? That will be nice." His mam broached, peering at him to gauge his reaction.

Rhys started to wash the ware, making sure to roll up the sleeves of his zippy first. He kept looking at the suds in the sink. "Ya, we are. It will be good to spend some time with her, just me and her."

"You two were always thick as thieves. We were very lucky, your dad and me, our two children never once fought, and even if you disagreed, a cup of tea always sorted it. And music. I know Andi has missed you lately."

Rhys stopped what he was doing, resting his hands on the edge of the sink as he dropped his head and sighed. "I know, mam, I know. I know it's all my fault and I've ben hurting her, hurting you guys. But I'm trying. I'm really fucking trying."

Jesus, he sounded pathetic, didn't he?

Shaking his head when his mam tried to soothe him, Rhys finished washing up, dried, and put the ware away. His head started to pound, tension flooding his veins as he said goodbye to his dad, then thanked his mam for dinner, promising to come back again.

"Though not every week, ma. I'd end up fat and lazy."

His mam had laughed, pleased to have fed him as she walked him to the door, handing him a bag of food. Rhys took it, then opened the door, and when he did his heart sank and his stomach flip-flopped.

Andi and Declan were standing on the other side of the door, and they both looked as surprised as Rhys felt when they spotted Rhys at the door.

"Oh," Andi started, her eyes darting from Declan to Rhys. "We were out for a drive and said we'd pop in. I got some cheesecake from that bakery you like, ma."

Rhys wasn't sure exactly what to do now, because this was the first time he and Declan had seen each other since he had left the retreat and Rhys felt himself bristle as Declan took stock of him. The calmness that Rhys had basked in lately evaporated like a puff of smoke as he bent to kiss his ma on the cheek.

"I was just leaving."

Both Andi and Declan stepped back to let him out of the house, Rhys only stopping when Andi reached for him. "We still on for lunch this week? Or dinner if that suits you better?"

Rhys flashed his sister a grin. "Looking forward to it. Let me know when you can fit me in."

Andi studied him, as if she wanted to make sure that he meant it, her eyes brightened when she realized that he did. Rhys inclined his head to Declan as he walked down the garden path, his heart hammering inside in his chest.

Holy awkwardness, Batman.

"Rhys?"

Angling his body slightly, Rhys turned back to see Declan halfway down the path, and Rhys wasn't sure he could handle another confrontation today, especially in front of his sister and his mam.

"You need a lift? I can drop ya back to yours."

Rhys understood that Declan was trying to open the lines of communication, trying to re-establish their friendship and even though Rhys hadn't been sure how to go about approaching Declan to find out if he was still in the band or not, or even if somehow, their friendship was salvageable, Rhys knew he wasn't ready just yet to find out.

Rhys held up the bag of food. "Nah, I'm good. Gotta walk off the dinner. Helps clear my head."

Declan frowned, looked like he wanted to say something more, thought better of it, and he just nodded in reply before heading back up the path. It was the most civil conversation they had had in months and yet still it felt like the chasm between them was growing bigger.

"Dec," Rhys called out, pain in his chest as Declan slowly turned to face him again. "Thanks for the offer, man. I appreciate it."

There was no hiding the utter shock and disbelief in Declan's features as Rhys waved to his mam and sister, and headed down the road, pulling his headphones from his jeans pocket and popping them into his ears, letting the music wash over him as he walked.

His chest ached so much that he wondered if he was having a panic attack. He made it to the end of the road, then Rhys rounded the corner, leaning against the concrete wall as he tried to steady the irregular rhythm in his heartbeat. His fingers twitched, playing the keys of a song until Rhys felt like he could breathe once more.

A car drove past and he could see the passengers turning as if they recognised Rhys, so he pushed off the wall and pulled up his hood, not feeling able to deal with the pretence of being Rhys Collins, member of Heartache Melody. He just wanted to be Rhys...if only for a little while.

Shay doesn't just see you as a rockstar....

The voice inside his head made him smile as he thought of the extremely sexy tattoo shop manager who didn't even realize that Rhys existed. There was no way Shay would even consider him in any way other than friendship, and maybe that made it so easy to talk to her...

But Rhys noticed just how drop-dead gorgeous Shay was, how self-assured she was and that made Rhys feel more attracted to her. And yet, it was safer for him to admire her in secret because Shay wasn't the kind of woman who would settle for a sort of reformed manwhore with more issues than *Vogue.*

He'd have more chance of making amends with Declan than trying to charm Shay Gleeson.

And to Rhys, neither option sounded at all enticing.

CHAPTER ELEVEN

Shay

SHAY WAS a hair's breadth away from committing murder.

She could probably argue justifiable homicide, considering the three stooges had been driving her up the walls all morning, and messing about, and even Cathal, who'd laughed at the start was beginning to have his patience exasperated.

What had started out as a morning where all four of them had gathered to showcase their ideas for their portion of the wall, had resulted in Darren whipping off his shirt and using the bloody paint to outline his design on himself. Then Isaac had started to paint like he was twelve and draw a dick on Darren's back.

They were nowhere near finalizing things and the entire shop was being gutted tomorrow as well as the upstairs living spaces. Shay had asked Cathal if he had settled on what extra living space he wanted. But Cathal had sighed and told Shay he didn't know what to do because he didn't need any more space.

And then her friend had flushed when Shay had pointed out that Luna probably had a ton of clothes and make-up. The boys then started to tease Cathal about asking Luna to move in, and that would be great for the shop because Cathal was always more relaxed after Luna stayed over.

That had resulted in Cathal throwing paint at the lads, and of course, they were only too happy to engage in a paint fight that had left them covered in paint and laughing like the fucking children they were.

Shay had started to try and pull them back in line, then Darren had flicked his paintbrush at Shay and that was when she had nearly committed murder.

Cathal had seemed to sense it, so he sent her out to get some coffee over at Rebel Books, telling her to sit and drink hers at the bookshop before coming back and he would make sure the place was sorted, and the idiots cleaned up.

She had stormed off then, grabbing her sketch-book and a pen, muttering under her breath that MJ was more mature than they were sometimes, and that made Isaac laugh in agreement.

So, Shay had ordered the largest coffee from

Cliona, one of the managers of Rebel Books, and went to the farthest table beside a window and sat down with a huff. She kicked off her shoes and pulled her legs up on the armchair, like she had done many times before, and balanced her sketchpad on her knees.

Her sketchpad had been filled lately with half-finished sketches of a rockstar who seemed to invade her thoughts. Despite Sinéad's advice, Shay found herself consumed by thoughts of Rhys and her drawings were proof of that. Over the last few days, Shay had drawn lots of pictures of a faceless man playing piano, another one of two men on stage, one shirtless and the other with a fake smile on his face. No matter how many sketches she did, Shay couldn't bring herself to finish the facial features because that would be akin to admitting that she had become a little obsessed lately.

Flipping over the pages, Shay began to work on her design for the wall. Cathal had decided to go for old school skull black and grey design with his, Darren had decided he wanted to do a trash polka design and Isaac wanted to use bold colours. Then Cathal had looked at Shay expecting her to show off her design, but considering Cathal was one of the best Japanese artists she'd ever seen, Shay was a little terrified to show him her take on a phoenix.

It wasn't exactly traditional, more fantastical, her phoenix the same colour as eyes that haunted her dreams, the mystical bird flying out from flames that morphed into claws as if they were reaching out of the depths of hell to drag the phoenix back to the flames.

"That's cool."

Shay snapped her head up, eyes widening when Rhys grinned back at her, his amber eyes filled with mischief. It was as if her thoughts had conjured him into being as Shay stole a look at him under her lashes.

Dressed in ripped faded jeans that hung low on his hips, moulded to his lean frame, and a grey tee that had music notes printed across the chest, Rhys looked like he could be modelling designer clothing rather than standing in a bookshop, looking at her with those fucking eyes of his.

"I did call your name but you seemed miles away. I get like that sat behind a piano."

Shay was at a loss for words when Rhys indicated to the chair across from her. "Can I sit?"

Nodding her head, Shay closed her sketchbook and set it aside, taking a sip of her coffee to gather her thoughts before she asked. "What are you doing here?"

Rhys glanced around and cocked a brow. "Would you believe me if I said I was looking for a book to read?"

Before Shay could reply, Rhys leaned back in his chair with a grin. "Nah, don't even bother coming out with a dumbass rockstar joke. I make um all the time. And considering I'm dyslexic, you'll only feel embarrassed after."

Despite the grin curving his lips into a devilish

smile, Shay could see Rhys brace himself for her to remark on his learning difficulties. Instead, Shay rested her chin on her knees.

"Is it reading you have difficulty with or writing? I've heard audiobooks are a great alternative and considering how easy music comes to you, the listening might help if you want to listen to a book."

Rhys blinked, sharp and sudden, as if he hadn't expected her to offer anything in response and Shay wondered if people either shied away from talking about it or they just lectured him on what he should be doing to help himself.

"I'd never considered audiobooks, but Niamh, Jameson's sister, she suggested it to me a couple of years ago and while I'm still not much of a reader, I do use it from time to time. And before you ask, I ordered some piano music from Niamh and came to collect them. I try to support her rather than go to a music shop."

Rhys leaned forward in his seat, leaning his elbows on his knees. "What brings you here?"

Shay let loose a sigh. "Cathal made me take a time out. I was ready to castrate one of them for being stupid idiots. So coffee..."

Barking out a laugh, Rhys asked for more details, and Shay gave him the very short and very boring story of the lads throwing paint at one another and then Darren had flicked his paintbrush at her and now she was here hoping the caffeine would sate her murderous intentions.

"Well, that explains it," Rhys began and time slowed as the man reached across the table and brushed his thumb over her cheek. Shay forgot how to breathe, and how to speak as heat flooded her body and she tried to still the rampant beating of her pulse.

"You've got some paint on your cheek," Rhys said, and maybe Shay was imagining it but his voice seemed to be lower, more husky than before and when Shay lifted her eyes to meet his, they clashed, and Shay saw a flicker of heat that seemed to set his amber eyes ablaze.

Rhys jerked his hand back suddenly, slumping back in his chair, and it was then and there that Shay was able to see the difference between a genuine smile and the fake-ass smile that he was now flashing her. Something had rattled Rhys, Shay considered as the rockstar got to his feet.

"I better go and collect my order. Try not to kill anyone today, Shay. I'd hate to have to visit you in prison."

Shay didn't even have the chance to offer her own goodbye, Rhys was already headed to the counter, either not noticing or oblivious to the admiring glances cast in his direction. Cliona handed him a bag and waved him off when he tried to pay, telling him that Jameson had already paid for them last night when they came in.

Rhys looked perplexed as he thanked Cliona, then glanced back to where Shay was sitting and offered her a salute before he ducked out the door and Shay deflated in her chair. Was she mad thinking that the heat in Rhys' eyes was for her? Had she lost utterly lost her mind to think that the connection between them had startled Rhys enough to make him react like he had?

Who the hell knew what was going through Rhys mind?

Who the hell knew what was going on inside her own head right now?

But it was something that snared Shay's thoughts long after her coffee had gone cold, long after she packed up her stuff and headed back to the tattoo shop, her thoughts so jumbled she forgot to bring coffee back for the lads, her expression so confused that even Cathal had asked if she was okay.

But Shay was far from okay... far from it.

CHAPTER TWELVE

Rhys

RHYS HAD BEEN CONFUSED as fuck after his encounter with Shay at Rebel Books. He would have bet anything that Shay wouldn't be interested in him, and yet, there had been a moment of charged energy between them that had frightened Rhys. It wasn't that he wasn't that he wasn't used to attraction...but lately, even before his unfortunate fall, Rhys had become jaded, tired of the mindless sometimes emptiness that washed over him during sex and it stopped being enjoyable.

Dr. Shannon had asked him to tell her why he felt the need to over indulge in drink and women, asking him why he felt the need to devalue himself by using his body to try and take from the fact that he was obviously unhappy.

It was why she had asked him to make a pledge with her, to respect himself enough to keep the progress that he had achieved by staying sober and celibate for the full ninety days. The therapist was smart enough to know that Rhys could have just lied his ass off and agreed to do what she wanted, but when she said that it was a challenge, Rhys felt like it was something he had to do for himself.

It had been a very long time since Rhys had felt like he had done anything for himself...

And then that one innocent touch of Shay's cheek had made Rhys want to abandon all his hard work and struggle and drag the woman to the nearest dark corner and fuck her senseless. He'd almost been able to taste her on his lips and he came very close to breaking.

And so Rhys had made a quick exit, the look on Shay's face telling him that he wasn't the only once confused. He could just be honest with her and tell Shay about his challenge, but the fear that Shay would laugh right in his face and mock him stopped him.

"It's all about breaking the habit, Rhys" Dr. *Shannon had told him. "It's about changing the self-destructive patterns and learning to like yourself. Once you do that, happiness is only a heartbeat away."*

Rhys had texted Jameson to thank him for the piano music, his bandmate replying instantly to say that there was no hassle, and maybe they could hang out and play some music whenever he had a chance. There was no hesitation in Rhys' answer, he just replied with a "sounds good, gimmie a shout when you're free", and Rhys felt like another bridge had started to be rebuilt.

His keyboard at home hadn't been enough to work on over the past week, but Rhys wasn't sure turning up at the studio was the best idea. At least at home, he could sing away and no one could hear him. Right now, Rhys didn't want to risk anyone finding out his secret before he was ready.

Shay had kept his secret though...

Rhys' mind kept wandering to Shay, and the keyboard sounds were starting to irritate him. Deciding he needed to walk to clear his head, Rhys grabbed his jacket and headed out, not sure why he took the piano music until his wander took him into the industrial estate where Declan's studio was.

Well, as long as I'm here.

Rhys let himself in, stopping to grab a water before he secluded himself in the large open space with his piano. The moment his fingers started to glide over the keys, Rhys felt the tension and stress leave his body and there was nothing but the music, the piano an extension of Rhys as he played.

Today Rhys didn't want slow and calming, he wanted to play until his fingers felt like they were bleeding and he was gasping for breath. Muse's *Sing for Absolution*, was the first song he played, pressing the keys a little harder than usual, then a second after he finished, Rhys moved on to Billie Eilish, *When the party's over,* giving it a harder rock feel that he liked to do with lots of songs.

He couldn't bring himself to sing today, the words caught in his throat as he played the final bars and lifted his fingers from the keys as he sucked in some air, as if his lungs hadn't dared to breathe throughout the song.

The silence rang in his ears and Rhys reached for the bottle of water, a prickling sensation on the nape of his neck alerting him that he was no longer alone.

The one person that Rhys had wanted to avoid stood in the doorway, amusingly standing in the same place as Andi had just over a week ago. Rhys drank half the bottle before setting it down on the floor, shifting his gaze back to where Declan was still standing.

"Hey."

Hey...that was all Declan said in greeting and for some reason that tiny word irked Rhys.

"Story." Rhys said in return, motioning toward the piano. "You need me to go so you can use it?"

"You and I both know that I can't do it justice, no matter how hard you tried to teach me."

The memory felt like an assault to his sanity, as Rhys recalled the many times he had sat down with Declan, painstakingly holding his hands as he tried to get him to play Twinkle Twinkle Little Star. It had taken a long time before Declan was any good, and

Rhys was reminded of how accomplished he had felt, teaching Declan to play.

Then they had shown Andi and she had offered to help as well.

"I should go," Rhys said, rising from behind the piano. "Will you tell Andi I'll see her for lunch tomorrow?"

Rhys crossed the room, ready to head out, glad when Declan stepped aside and Rhys passed him by, sheer stubbornness was the only reason why Rhys didn't lift his head and look at Declan.

"Has it really come to this? You can't even stand to be in the same fucking room as me? Do you despise me so much that you're just gonna flee every time I walk into a goddam room?"

To be fair, Declan sounded like he had finally come to the end of his rope and Rhys couldn't give him an answer as to when he might be ready. Or explain that it wasn't down to Declan; that Rhys had to sort his head out before he could sit down and tell Declan his feelings.

"For fuck sake, Rhys." Declan's gravely growl stopped Rhys from walking out. Instead, he turned to face Declan across the room.

"I promised your sister that I wouldn't get in your face, but you're killing me, Rhys. I finally have the woman I love, but I lost my best friend. I'm right back where I started arguing with a goddamn Collins and I don't know what I've done wrong."

Rhys let loose a harsh bitter laugh. "Of course, yet again, it's all about Declan Walsh, and nobody else fucking matters. You can't ever let things alone, can you? You pick and pick at the scab until it scars. The world doesn't revolve around you, Dec. It really fucking doesn't."

"I'm not saying it does, Rhys!" Declan yelled, running his hands through his hair. "The band mightn't survive this. Is that what you want, Rhys?"

His gut clenched at the reality of the predicament they were in. if Rhys couldn't get over his feelings toward Declan and Andi being together, then he may have to get used to the fact that maybe, he had to leave the band and that would obliterate Rhys.

"I want to ask Andi to marry me."

Declan's sentence hit him like bullets, confirmation that in the end, Declan had chosen Andi over Rhys and it was like confirmation of his greatest fears, that Declan had only been his friend to get to Andi. It was as if Declan was trying hard to hammer the final nail in their friendship and Rhys would let him.

"You don't need my permission, Dec. You'll do what you want to do in the end."

Declan shook his head. "You know Andi wouldn't say yes if she knows you still don't approve. How can either of us be happy when our best friend can't be happy for us? Are you that selfish?"

Rhys recoiled as if Declan had punched him, bile creeping up his throat and he wanted to up the badness that pooled in his stomach. "Yeah, I guess I am, Dec. If that makes you feel better."

Turning around so fast that Rhys felt dizzy, he strode from the room, and started walking as fast as he could, reaching up when he felt wetness on his face and realised he was crying.

What was the point in trying to make amends and be better? The people closest to him expected the worst from him so why not just live up to it?

Pulling his phone from his pocket, Rhys dialled a number, shutting down as he said into the phone. "Hey, it's Rhys. Where's the party at?"

CHAPTER THIRTEEN

Shay

SHAY WAS EXHAUSTED by the time she arrived back at her apartment, after a long day of helping out at the shop. The entire ground floor had been wiped out and rebuilt quite fast, much to Cathal's delight. New partitions were erected, giving six tattoo rooms at the back of the shop, and a new kitchen and hangout area. Cathal had made sure that the old counter, one that Barry had carved with his own hands had been kept, with a new entrance by way of a half door added to it.

Before any of the painting could be done, or furniture and equipment set into place, they had to clean from top to bottom. They had worked hard all day, with even Darren and Isaac concentrating to get shit done so they could take a day off tomorrow before they then get to painting and that.

The upstairs living area was still pending, and anytime Shay asked Cathal what the plan was, her friend brushed her off. Maybe he was considering asking Luna to move in with him?

Arriving home, Shay showered and changed into a comfy top and shorts, not bothering to do anything but fall into bed, deciding tomorrow's day off was time enough to tidy. Her head hit the pillow, sleep claiming her so fast that when her phone started to ring, Shay thought she was dreaming.

Groaning as she rolled over in the bed and grabbed her phone, pressed answer. The sound of music blaring in the background, the heavy thumping of the dance beat made Shay sit up in the bed and rub her eyes.

"Darren, I swear to fuck if you are calling for a lift or have butt dialled me because you're drunk, I'll skin ya alive."

Shay pulled the phone away from her ear, then glanced at the screen, and saw a number she didn't recognise. She was about to hang up, taking it as a wrong number when the sound of music suddenly dulled and she heard a door closing.

"It's Rhys."

The sadness in his tone made Shay sit up a little straighter. "Rhys? What's wrong?"

There was a brief pause and Shay checked her

phone to make sure the call was still connected, then she heard Rhys yell that the bathroom was occupied.

"Where are you, Rhys?"

"Would you laugh at me if I told ya I'm currently hiding out in some dude's bathroom because partying while sober isn't much fun?"

Jesus Christ...the last place Rhys needed to be was at a party. She wanted to know how he got her phone number, but it was more important to get Rhys out of the situation he was in so he didn't risk his recovery.

"I don't think I can make myself leave, Shay. I really want to get mind-numbingly drunk right now." Rhys admitted down the phone.

Shay was already getting out of bed when she replied. "I'll come get you."

"You're probably best off not, Shay. I'm toxic. I really shouldn't have called you."

Her heart clenched at the weight of the sadness in Rhys' tone, and even as she told him to send the address to her phone. She dressed quickly, heard her phone ping, and then the phone cut out.

Driving to the address that Rhys had sent her, Shay could hear the party going on from a mile away. Flashing lights and head-splitting music greeted her. She parked her car in the drive outside the house, then walked right in. Glancing around, Shay had stairs in front of her and a couple getting hot and heavy right in front of them.

To her left, people danced and to her right, the

kitchen had people filling up their drinks. The smell of weed was almost enough to make her eyes water. Not knowing where Rhys was, Shay took a chance and headed up the stairs, passing the couple making out, and started calling Rhys' name. She felt her heart sink at the thought that he'd already left and was somewhere drinking or worse, when a door opened and Rhys stood in the doorway, looking broken and hell, just sad.

"You ready to go?" Shay asked him, holding out her hand and he looked at her outstretched hand like he didn't know what she wanted him to do.

Rhys stepped out of the bathroom, slipped his ice-cold fingers into her hand and Shay sucked in some air at the electricity that shot up her hand at Rhys' touch, the same tingly feeling she had gotten when he had grazed her cheek with his thumb.

The rockstar said nothing as Shay guided him down the stairs and out the door. Rhys mutely got into the passenger seat, put on his seatbelt, and leaned his head against the window, closing his eyes. Shay started the car and was about to ask Rhys for his address to drop him home when she heard him say ever so quietly.

"I can't face being alone right now. The silence is killing me."

Well, Shay couldn't drive him home now, could she? She could never have it on her conscious if she dropped Rhys off at his house and he went and did something stupid. He trusted her enough to call her and ask for her help. What had happened to push him so close to the edge?

And just when Shay would have asked him about what happened, Rhys reached out and turned the radio up a little, a wry smile making Shay's heart skip a beat as he hummed away to the song.

They didn't speak after that, not even when Shay parked her car outside her apartment building, not even when they both got out of the car and Shay led them upstairs to her apartment. For a brief moment, Shay worried that some paparazzi had followed them and she would end up in the papers, just like Cathal had when he first started dating Luna. They may have called Cathal a reformed young offender, but Shay was the daughter of a notorious gangland solicitor; it could ruin Rhys' career.

The man in question walked with a stiffness that Shay had never seen from him before. His eyes looked distant. The spark that usually lit up those amber eyes of his completely shut down as Shay told him to take off his jacket. She fixed him some tea, Rhys holding it for a few minutes before setting it down on the table.

"You wanna tell me what happened?" Shay broached, hoping to get some answers because it hurt her seeing him like this.

Rhys got to his feet and went to the window, looking out into the night so Shay couldn't see his face. "I had a fight with Declan." Rhys finally said, his shoulders slumping. "I can't fix what's broken between us. I don't think there's even a point."

Shay opened her mouth to respond, to tell Rhys it couldn't be that bad but he just turned and walked right passed her, into the bedroom, pulled off his top, and flopped down on her bed, he started snoring a few minutes later and Shay slumped against the breakfast bar, reaching for her phone as she glanced at the clock, wondering who she should call.

Cathal answered her on the fourth ring, yawning down the phone as he said. "Shay, everything okay?"

"I'm not sure. Are you with Luna?" Shay asked quietly, unsure how deep Rhys was asleep.

"I'm putting you on speaker."

Once she heard Luna's voice, Shay explained about Rhys' phone call and that he was asleep at her place.

"Is he high or drunk?" Luna asked, concern in her tone.

"Surprisingly no," Shay admitted, inhaling a breath. "He just seemed so sad, defeated even. He hasn't said much to be fair, just enough. He told me he had a fight with Declan, that he couldn't fix things between them and that he didn't think there was a point in even trying."

"That doesn't sound like Rhys."

No, it really didn't.

"Do you need me to come get him?" Luna continued, but Shay glanced toward her bedroom knowing if

Luna showed up right now, then it might feel like a betrayal to Rhys.

"No, he's grand. Leave him sleep and I'll call if I need help. Maybe call his sister and tell her he's here, in case she worries."

Shay heard Luna go off to make her own call, as Cathal came back on the line. "Shay, you good?"

Was she? Shay didn't really have an honest answer for Cathal right now so she just told him that she was and that she would call him again if she needed him. They hung up, and Shay went to stand in the doorway to her bedroom and watched Rhys toss and turn.

When he finally settled, Rhys lay facing her, the shadows cast from the streetlight outside making his features sharper, like glass, that made her want to get her sketchpad and draw Rhys as he slept...there was a beauty in the darkness that surrounded him.

Shay sighed, shaking herself from her thoughts and ironically she would have laughed considering her attraction to Rhys. But this wasn't exactly how she fantasied having a rockstar in her bed.

CHAPTER FOURTEEN

Rhys

RHYS WOKE IN AN UNFAMILIAR BED, stretching out his long limbs as he sat up and rubbed his eyes. Memories of yesterday came back to haunt him. Jesus, had he really been so pathetic that he had called up Shay and asked her to come get him because he was such a sad mess?

Rolling out of the bed, Rhys slipped on his shoes and grabbed his tee from where he had thrown it last night, yanking it over his head as he emerged from the bedroom to see Shay watching him with a careful expression. Although, she couldn't mask the way her eyes wandered over him as he righted his tee and leaned against the counter.

"Hey." He said in greeting then mentally cursed himself.

Hey? Smooth, asshole, very smooth.

Shay slid a mug over to him, then popped two slices of bread into the toaster. "I'm not much of a cook so toast is what you get. Cathal tried to teach me but the food I can cook doesn't extend to breakfast."

Shay smiled as she said it, looking at him with dark eyes as Rhys lifted his mug to lips, his own eyes subtly roaming over the slim but curvy woman. Her skin was pale, a stark contrast to her black hair, which was streaked with little strands of purple. The jeans she wore seemed like they had been moulded to her form and Rhys wondered if her ass would be firm in his grasp or soft.

Turning then and shielding her ass from his view, Shay folded her arms across her chest, pushing the perfect handfuls up, almost spilling from her string top. An array of tattoos was inked on her arms, dipping down underneath her clothing, and Rhys wanted to strip Shay so he could see what other ink she had hidden.

"Eyes to my face, rockstar."

Rhys grinned as he did what he was told, offering a smile in apology, the flush to Shay's skin making him consider she might have enjoyed his eyes on her. But that was a conversation for another day and Rhys had already made a fool of himself in the last twenty-four hours.

"Sorry." He said, trying to look sheepish and that made Shay laugh and Rhys liked the sound of her laughter.

"You are not in the least bit sorry, Rhys Collins, so don't act all sweet and innocent with me." Shay plated the toast that had just popped and pushed it toward him, along with a knife and some butter. "Now eat your damn breakfast so you can't complain I let you starve."

Rhys proceeded to butter his toast, taking a bite as Shay walked around the counter and then hoisted herself up near him as she reached over and took a piece of his toast and ate it, shrugging when Rhys cocked a brow at her.

Shay was close enough for him to reach out and touch, the itch on his palms to do just that, and it took a fair amount of willpower to eat his toast and not act on his urge. She leaned back on her hands and regarded him, those dark brown eyes seemed to look into his soul.

"So, you want to talk about last night or are we just gonna ignore what happened?"

"Ignore it?" Rhys ventured, carning an eye roll from Shay.

"Listen," she began, and Rhys knew she wasn't about to bullshit him or placate him. "We can dance around the fact that you nearly ruined all the progress that you had achieved by putting yourself in a situation you should have been miles away from, or you can get it off your chest exactly what made you want to get blind ass drunk to forget."

Rhys let loose a croak of laughter. "Damn, Shay, I can see why you rule Rebel Ink with an iron fist. I'm feeling like a jackass already. You could leave my balls where they are and save me some shred of dignity."

The slow, sexy, smile that curved Shay's very kiss-able lips made desire pool in Rhys stomach. "I think you'll survive."

Arching her brows in question, as if to tell Rhys she was waiting for him to go on, Rhys huffed out an exasperated breath. "It's not a big deal. I had a fight with Declan. It's par for the course at the moment, so ya... he said some things and so did I and we parted with him basically calling me a selfish prick, which isn't a lie and I think I'm out of a job."

Shay narrowed her gaze as she looked at him. "Declan won't fire you. I mean, he can't can he?"

Rhys shrugged, drinking more of his coffee before he responded. "Declan can do whatever the hell he wants. If he decides to walk, then Heartache Melody is over. His voice is gold. They can find another keyboard player. I'm replaceable. Dec's not."

For the longest moment, Shay just starred at him. Rhys edged a little closer, until their fingers were a ghost of a touch away, and when Shay spoke, Rhys didn't want to imagine the huskier timbre of her tone.

"Why do you do that? Why do you run yourself down like that?"

"I'm not running myself down, Shay," Rhys replied. "I'm just realistic to my place in the band. I play the keyboard. Declan and Jamie write the songs and Luna, her drums skills are second to none, she basically sells herself. Out of the four of us, I'm just the eye candy."

His last remark was meant to elevate the seriousness of the conversation, but Shay was looking at him like she couldn't believe a word he had just said or the fact that he actually believed it.

She tilted her chin up to look at him and it was like a magnet pulling Rhys to her, his hand cupping the side of her face as he lowered his face towards Shay's lips. He felt the sharp intake of her breath against his skin.

"It's all about breaking the habit, Rhys. It's about changing the self-destructive patterns and learning to like yourself. Once you do that, happiness is only a heartbeat away."

Rhys jerked back before his lips could capture Shay's, taking a step back and from the look on Shay's face, she was as shocked by his sudden retreat as he was. His chest heaved and his heart was fucking galloping inside his chest. Shay's cheeks went red as she pushed off the counter and turned away from him. He wanted to turn her around so she was looking at him as he tried to explain.

"I think you should go, Rhys." There was no masking the hurt in Shay's tone. His rejection had stung her...he could hear it in her tone but Rhys wanted to kiss her so badly his body *ached*. He needed to make sure Shay knew it was nothing to do with her and it had everything to do with him and his issues.

"I want to kiss you so bad," He started, willing Shay to turn and look at him. "I want to peel off your clothes so I can taste the ink on your skin. If you don't believe anything else that I say, believe me when I tell you that if I had kissed you, I'd not stop with just a taste."

Shay angled her body so that she was looking at him again, and before she could ask him to leave again, he told her about his promise. "When I was at the retreat, the therapist, she told me I use drink and sex to push down what I'm feeling. I'm self-destructive apparently and I made a pact with her that I would go ninety days without reverting back to form. I have to see it through, Shay. I need to prove to myself that I can. Please understand."

Shay didn't say anything in reply, so Rhys grabbed his hoody and headed for the door, halting only when Shay grabbed his arm. The charge between them was still there, but Shay inclined her head. "Stay. I've got the day off so you can hang out with me for a while if you want."

Removing her hand, Shay walked over to the chair by the window and curled herself into it, picking up her sketchpad and averting her gaze from Rhys. The relief that washed over him was palpable, as he followed Shay over to the living room and sat down on the couch across from her, content to sit there and watch her work for a time, nothing but the silence between them, and for the first time in forever, the silence didn't haunt him as much as it tended to do.

"*Happiness is only a heartbeat away.*"

Rhys snorted, and then Shay glanced up at him, and he offered her a smile, and she returned it, then went back to her drawing and Rhys could see himself spending mornings like this, with Shay, content in the silence.

CHAPTER FIFTEEN

Rhys

RHYS WATCHED Shay sketch for a half an hour before he broke the veil of silence that was comfortable between them, Shay lost in her own world, a look of concentration on her face that Rhys felt mirrored his own when he worked on music.

"Whatcha working on?" he asked, leaning forward, resting his chin on his fist as she lifted her gaze to his.

"Just some tattoo designs. Nothing much."

"Can I see? It's okay if you don't want to show me but since I can't draw a straight line, I'm fascinated at the shit some artists can draw."

Rhys let her consider it, keeping his lips firmly shut in case opening his mouth would prevent her from showing him what she was working on. Slowly, shyly even, Shay lifted her sketch book and turned it around so he could see. The image on the paper hit Rhys like a punch to the gut.

Shay's artwork featured an eye that Rhys knew had to be his, the amber much brighter than his own or at least he thought so. The eye had a sheen of wetness, like it was crying and the tears that fell from the eyes were not actual tears, but music notes. Behind the eye was bursts of colour, and sheet music and Rhys just knew that Shay had drawn this about him.

Never had he felt such a strong over emotion as he did looking at the drawing on Shay's sketchpad. He felt as if Shay had seen past the persona and was looking at him, who he really was. He needed this piece of art in his life, whether it was on his skin or hanging in his place.

"If you hate it, I can throw it out."

"No," Rhys said, aware his voice sounded a little harsh, a little hard. "No. I want it...when it's done. Will you tattoo it on me?"

Shay held the sketchpad to her chest, shaking her head. "You can have it but I'm not a tattoo artist, Rhys. I know Cathal or any of the other lads would love to ink that for you."

It was Rhys' turn to shake his head. "No. I want you to do it. Doesn't have to be anytime soon but you drew it, you deserve to be the one to ink me. Besides, I'd much rather look at you than any of the lads."

"Rhys, I can see from your face how much you want the artwork. I may never get to apprentice. You know that." Shay offered him a sad smile. "But I won't charge you for the design...I'm sure getting to tattoo a rockstar will be a novelty for the lads. Cathal might do it on the daily, but Isaac and Darren would kill to do it. talk with them and you'll get a feel for who works for you."

Shay Gleeson worked for him. But he would wait.

"And is that what you wanna do with your life, Shay? Do you wanna settle when one simple conversation could make it happen?"

Shay closed her sketchpad and set it on the arm of the couch beside her. "Do you wanna settle for just being a keyboard player? Don't you want people to know that you can sing? Do you wanna settle when once simple conversation could make it happen?"

Her words were sharp, like razers, tossed back at him like she was firing shots and Rhys took it, because he had opened the door and Shay had firmly slammed it back in his face. Holding up his hands, Rhys grinned, as Shay continued to glare at him.

"To answer your question and maybe give ya some context, singing is the only thing I have that is mine, that I don't have to share with anyone, but you it seems. I love playing the keys, it's the one time that I feel like I'm not failing at something and not competing ... and that's a stretch at the moment. Is it wrong to just want something that belongs to me and no one else?"

Rhys shut his eyes, felt the prick of tears and there was no way in hell he was gonna blubber in front of Shay. He was trying to be fucking honest and he really should keep his fucking mouth shut.

"I'm afraid."

Prying his eyes open, he looked at Shay as she continued. "I've always been good at art and I've always wanted to tattoo, but what if I'm no good at it? what if I can't put all the knowledge I have in my head from working at Rebel Ink into practise and I make an ass of myself? I don't want Cathal to have to tell me that I'm shite, or just lying his ass off and tell me I'm making progress because we are family."

Rhys could understand her fear; he had a fair amount of it himself.

"If I fail," Shay continued, wrapping her arms around herself in a way that made Rhys want to comfort her. "Then my dad was right and he would relish in it. He told me it was beneath me to want to be a tattoo artist, that I should strive to be more, to be like him, and I could never let him gloat like that. And if I'm shit, then he would be delighted."

"Declan opens his mouth and honey comes out. Andi sings and the world stops rotating to listen to them. When Andi sits behind a piano and sings, like nothing else you've every heard. Before my voice changed, I knew I could never live up to them so I pretended my voice breaking meant I lost my singing ability. I was afraid of being compared to them and feeding into my inferiority complex."

Shay regarded him for the longest time, as if she was trying out just how genuine his words were, and then she let loose a chortle of laughter. "For fuck sake, we're a well met pair, aren't we?"

Rhys shrugged in response, grinning as he said. "Misery loves company, right?"

Returning his grin, Shay unfurled her arms from around her stomach, then tilted her head like she'd had an idea. "How do you feel about another challenge?"

"Well, considering how close I came to kissing you earlier, I'm not doing very well on that challenge, but sure, why the fuck not?"

Rhys liked the sparkle of mischief in Shay's eyes as she put her feet on the floor and leaned in toward him. "Let's work toward sharing our secrets. If you promise to tell everyone that you can sing, then I will tell Cathal I want to start training as an apprentice. We do it together so we both have support when we might back away from it. It might help you mend fences with Declan, and it might force me to be brave."

While he wasn't one hundred percent sure that telling Declan that he had lied for years and could hold a tune was the best way to start to mend things between them, he would do anything to help Shay reach her own dreams. When she held out her hand, he took it, shaking it and she quickly pulled it back, though she had a smile on her face.

"I guess that's settled."

"I guess it is. But I meant what I said, Shay. If I do get that tattooed, I want you to do it. And I might never be ready to tell everyone bout the singing. But I will promise to try and that has to be enough, okay?"

Shay nodded in agreement and then reclined in her chair. "Right, so that's settled, do you plan on hanging out with me all day or have you got your own shit to do?"

Rhys arched a brow, unable to stop his lips from curving. "Trying to get rid of me already?"

"Not at all...but if I have to feed you for the rest of the day, then you can order take out just saying."

Rhys glanced at his watch. "I was supposed to meet, Andi for lunch. I could rain check?"

"Nah, go have lunch with your sister and text me and let me know how it went. Since you have my number it seems...how did you get my number?"

He wasn't about to admit that he had asked Jameson for her number when he texted him to say thanks for the music booking his bandmate that he had promised to send Shay some tracks for the shop playlist, but had forgot to get her number.

Jameson had just sent a text with Shay's number, telling Rhys he was losing his touch.

Rhys got to his feet and tapped his nose. "I gotta keep some mystery. You nearly know all my secrets,

Shay Gleeson. How else will I make sure you keep hanging out with me?"

Rolling her eyes, Shay rose off the chair and gave him a mock shove towards the door and Rhys laughed, asking Shay if she treated all her celebrity friends like him.

"There's no one like you, Rhys Collins, now get out of my gaff before I kick you out."

Chapter Sixteen

Shay

SHAY FOUND herself alone with Cathal the next day, the two of them arriving at the shop early to start to get stuff sorted before Darren arrived to help out. Isaac had MJ for the day, but he was going to pop in later on with her. Shay always loved when MJ came to the shop; she liked being an auntie and spoiling the little girl as much as possible.

Growing up, Shay had always wanted a sibling, someone she could fuss over and teach things too, but her parents had never seemed inclined to have another child after seeing how much disruption even one child could have on their busy social calendar. Shay had raised herself really, and the only family she had really known until she met the boys was Sinéad, and she'd been devastated when Sinéad had left for Spain and the communication had become sparse over the years.

Of course, Sinéad had her reasons, and now that Shay was fully aware of what Sinéad had gone through, it had made sense for Sinéad's mother Matilda to get her away from the situation. That being said, Shay was glad to have her best friend back in her life and sticking around Cork for the foreseeable now that she was dating Jameson Kent.

Thinking of Jameson made Shay think about Rhys, but then she had been thinking about him a lot of the last couple of days. They had texted on and off, with Rhys telling her that things had gone surprisingly well with his sister, probably because they both made a point of not bringing up Declan during the time they were together. And Rhys hadn't mentioned his near miss with the party.

Shay had told him he needed to be upfront with people when he was struggling and ask for help, to which Rhys had replied and said, he'd called her, hadn't he?

The drollness of his retort made Shay smile as she looked over her phoenix that had turned out epically. There was hammering and sawing going on upstairs, as Cathal came back into the newer part of Rebel Ink, a mug of coffee in each hand. He handed one off to her, then leaned against the counter and regarded her with a look that made Shay feel like she was back in school.

"What?" she asked before taking a sip of her coffee and quirking an eyebrow. "Have I got something on my face or what? You're staring at me."

Cathal was quiet for a few minutes, his brow furrowed in the way it did when her friend was thinking too much. He released a sigh, set his coffee down, and folded his arms across his chest. "So, you and Rhys?"

"Me and Rhys what?"

Shay knew where Cathal was going with the conversation because Shay had also been all up in Cathal's business when he had started showing an interest in Luna. But Shay didn't know how to define what was going on with her and Rhys just yet, so she had nothing much to share.

"He stayed over the other night."

Rolling her eyes as she shook her head. "Jesus, Cathal, I didn't know I needed permission to have someone stay over at my house. He needed help so I helped him."

"Making sure Rhys is okay is not your responsibility."

Shay blinked in surprise at the sharpness in Cathal's tone. "Really? This coming from the guy who literally chased off a knife welding mugger and started to date the rockstar he rescued? I'm surprised at you Cathal."

A muscle in Cathal's jaw ticked and Shay knew she had hit a sore spot. "Why the sudden interest,

Cathal? Luna wants to know what's going on with Rhys?"

"Can I not just be worried about you? Is that a crime now?"

Shay had no idea why the hell Cathal was getting so defensive when he had brought it up!

"Of course, you can be worried about me, Cathal. But I'm just a little confused why my friendship with Rhys had gotten your knickers in a twist."

"And that's all ye are, friends?" Cathal continued to push and Shay was just about done with his attitude for today.

"For fuck sake, Cathal. If you wanna know if I'm fucking him, then just come out and ask me and cut the bullshit. And to answer your question, no, we are not sleeping together. Considering you and me have been friends for years and never once even considered getting naked, I would have thought you of all people would not be such a hypocrite."

Cathal's face pinched into frown. "Jesus, Shay, I'm trying to protect you. Rhys is going through some stuff and I know you always had a thing for him before you knew him. I just want to make sure you are looking at this with a clear head and not as someone with-"

"With what, Cathal?" Shay interrupted, setting her own mug down before she threw it at the idiot's head. "Like a fangirl who hops into bed with the rockstar because he is one. You think that little of me?"

Throwing his hands up in the air, Cathal huffed.

"Why the hell are we fighting over this? I just wanted to make sure you were okay and you're making a big deal about me just checking in. I don't want you to get hurt, Shay."

"Well, you can stop worrying because we are just friends. I'm an outsider who he can talk to without the need to take sides. And I think if it bugs you so much, then maybe we shouldn't talk about it. Maybe we should put that area of discussion off the table."

Running his hand through his hair, Cathal was still frowning as he regarded Shay. "I don't know how this turned into us having and argument and I want you to talk to me, Shay. We don't not talk to each other. No matter what, we have each others backs. I'm just trying to look out for you."

Shay felt her heart squeeze, but she felt like there was something else lurking with Cathal's questioning. "Do you think I'm not good enough for him? Are you the only one who can date or be friends with rockstars?"

Cathal had the good sense to look horrified by her questions. "Fuck no, Shay. I don't think Rhys is good enough for you. From what I know, he's rash, and impulsive, and has a major chip on his shoulder. You normally hate guys like that."

"Maybe you have him all wrong," Shay replied with a shrug. "Maybe the cockiness is a front for an insecurity. Maybe the attitude is a front. Your girl-friend was known as a maneater and a party animal and you still wanted to see beyond all that. Don't get judgy."

Tilting his head to the side, Cathal said. "Okay, I get the point. But I really do just want to make sure you don't get hurt, Shay. Rhys hasn't been making good choices lately and I don't want you to get dragged into all that. And I really do think that Rhys is punching above his weight if he is trying to pursue you."

The last sentence was said with a little smile, with Cathal trying to alleviate the tension between them, the two of them working in silence until Darren came in, took one look at the two of them and raised a brow at Cathal, who just shrugged and continued with what they were doing.

Shay understood that Cathal was just looking out of her, like she would do for him. She felt like she needed to make sure that he knew that. Even when they'd had a disagreement with each other before, it had never left her with such a bitter taste in her mouth. Darren kept looking from Cathal to her, then back again, and he almost opened his mouth to say something when Isaac and MJ arrived.

MJ came over to give Shay a hug, and Shay indulged in an extra big hug. Dressed in a brand new Heartache Melody logo tee, a pink and black tartan skirt with black tights and brand new converse high tops, the little girl grinned when Shay asked her if Luna had bought her the outfit.

"She got me the t-shirt," MJ explained, and like it was nothing unusual continued, "But Oli sent me the shoes and clothes. He's my friend."

Shay got to her feet and looked at the little girl's dad, the bemused expression on Isaac's face as he just shrugged. "Hell if I know what's going on. Rockstars dating my boss, rockstars and F1 drivers buying MJ stuff. The world's gone fucking mental, Shay. At least I can trust you to have the good sense to stay away from rockstars and famous people."

Shay rolled her eyes, ignoring the look she got from Cathal as she went about her day, and although they didn't speak about it for the rest of the day, Shay expected this wasn't the last she would her about it from Cathal.

CHAPTER SEVENTEEN

Shay

YOU'VE SPENT an awful long time getting ready for a group get together.

Shay chastised herself for feeling so out of sorts as she tried to decide on what to wear to the impromptu get together tonight. She hadn't been sure that she even should go when Cathal asked her, but then Rhys had texted and asked her if she was going, that he wouldn't go if she wasn't there for back up. Then he had sent her a selfie of him pouting and it had made her laugh, so she told the idiot that she would go.

The little get together was being held at Luna's family pub, her dad agreeing to close the back room for the night when the band had offered to pay for the night's takings. Shay was worried Rhys being in a pub might not be the best place if he wanted to stay sober for his ninety days, but she wasn't his mother and all she could do is be there with him if he found it all too much.

Rhys had offered to come get her, however Cathal had also offered and showing up with Rhys might be enough to start the gossiping. Plus, Shay and Cathal needed to clear the air, since things had been awkward for the last week, before they had to face other people. There was no way she was going to air her dirty laundry in public and Cathal wouldn't want that either.

So the dilemma of what to wear drove her half mad for the day as she ransacked her wardrobe. She'd been so paranoid that Cathal would think she was dressing up for Rhys, that she had texted Sinéad to ask her what she was planning in wearing. When Shay saw how casual Sinéad was going, Shay decided to say fuck it and just wear black jeans, a vest and throw on a red and black check shirt over it.

She left her hair loose and added a little more make up then she did at the shop, choosing to wear sneakers instead of heels because it wasn't going to be that kind of night. Shay was already waiting outside her building when Cathal pulled up in a taxi.

Getting in to the back with Cathal, she smiled at her boss and said. "Thanks for collecting me. I assumed Luna would need help getting set up."

"Nah," Cathal said with a grin. "Luna roped Luke into helping since he was missing Emil. He's away on international duty this week and Luke had to stay to work on his rally car for the next season."

Shay knew it must be hard for Luna's brother to spend so much time away from his footballer boyfriend, but she also knew that Sinéad also missed Jameson when he was away with the band. Even Cathal missed Luna when she was away despite the fact he joked that his world was a lot quieter when Luna was away.

"So, do we know who else is gonna be there tonight? Are we expecting your tattoo fanboy to rock up unexpectedly?"

Cathal chuckled shaking his head. "Oli's going mad he can't come but he does want to book in for another session on his rib piece when he can free up some time. I think he mentioned coming back to Ireland in the next couple months."

"Guaranteed he doesn't last that long." Shay laughed, leaning back in the seat.

"Then it's just the band, Noah and Quinn from the Rebel Racers crew...then me and you."

"Where are dumb and dumber tonight?" Shay asked, referring to Darren and Isaac, listening as Cathal told her Darren had a last minute family thing and Isaac decided to stay at home with Melody.

"Isaac needs to get out more. He's such a good dad, like. He shouldn't put his life on hold. MJ"'s old enough now if he wanted to start dating someone knew."

"I think Isaac is scared." Cathal told her and Shay had to agree. MJ's mam was Isaac first love and she had broken Isaac's heart in the way she chose drugs over her daughter. The woman hadn't seen MJ in over two years after a relapse and Isaac was happy to keep MJ away from all that.

They arrived at the Sullivan pub a few minutes later and after getting out, Cathal placed a hand on her elbow when she made to head inside. She paused, lifting her gaze up to Cathal.

"Are we good, Shay?" Cathal asked, letting go of her arm. "I've felt shite all week since we argued. I'm sorry."

Shay gave Cathal a smile and mock punched him. "I'm sorry too. Let's just forget all about it, okay? We're good."

The relief on Cathal's face was palpable as he led her in to the pub, waving at Luna's dad as they made their way to the back room, where Shay could hear the party had already started to get going. Cathal left her to go and give Luna a kiss, clapping her twin brother on the back, as the two set up a mic stand behind a massive piano.

Jameson and Sinéad were off to the side, with Sinéad sitting on her boyfriend's lap. The moment she saw Shay standing there, Sinead waved her over to where they were. Shay started to make her way toward the couple, when she heard a velvet voice say in her ear.

"You really gonna just leave me standing here by my lonesome?"

Shay glanced to the side as Rhys stepped up beside her, dressed in all black, making his pale skin seemed almost white. He grinned over at her, nudged her shoulder. "Everyone's looking to see what you do. Personally, I think you should sing my praises, really mess with their heads."

Instead, Shay barked out a laugh and smacked Rhys hard on the arms. "Shup, dumbass. Come on, let's go sit with Sinéad and Jameson."

Not even thinking too much on it, Shay grabbed Rhys' hand and dragged him over to where Sinéad watched her with open curiosity. Jameson and Rhys bumped fists, with Rhys declining a beer when Luna came over and asked what they wanted to drink.

"Just a coke, Luna. I drove my car over. I'm good."

They all chatted for a few minutes, then Luna squealed and ran over to hug her best friend Quinn, who arrived with Noah Donovan. Quinn and Noah were F1 drivers, with Noah narrowly missing out on his first drivers championship last year. Everyone was saying hello to each other, getting drinks and finishing setting up when Rhys suddenly went rigid beside her.

Shay glanced toward the door to where Rhys' sister, PR badass, Andi Collins walked hand in hand with Declan Walsh, the lead singer of Heartache

Melody. They were a striking pair, even dressed in casual clothes and Shay had the most inappropriate thought that those two would have really beautiful babies.

She nudged Rhys, pulling his eyes from the pair at the same time as Declan and Andi glanced in the younger Collins' direction. "Stop frowning. You'll give that okay-looking face wrinkles." She muttered under her breath, loud enough for only Rhys to hear her, and he let loose a chortle of laughter, before winking at Shay.

"Okay looking I can work with."

Damn, that look he was giving her was nearly enough for Shay to forget that they were in a room full of people who were studying them with curious eyes. Rhys relaxed into his chair, lifted his coke in greeting to Andi, who smiled warmly back at her brother.

The same thing couldn't be said for Declan though, who was glaring at Rhys like the devil himself was sitting in the room, and he only looked away when Andi said something sharply to him. He then stalked over to where Noah was holding out a beer to Declan.

"Well, this should be fun." Rhys said drooly to her, rubbing his hands on his jeans as he pointed at the makeshift stage. "If I'd known I'd have to spend the night listening to everyone sing, I might have stayed at home."

Rhys didn't bother to mask the bitterness in his tone, but Shay knew that it was only because he didn't feel like he could hold his nerve yet and get up on the stage and sing in front of the rest of the band.

"You could still play the piano, yano...if you didn't want to sing." Shay told him softly, flashing him and encouraging smile.

"Nah," Rhys sighed after taking a sip of his coke. "I'll stay for a bit and then make an Irish exit. Not like anyone will miss me anyways."

Well, there was no way Shay was going to waste the opportunity to help Rhys. He might be mad at first, but once he got up there and sang, it would take away some of the pain Rhys was carrying inside him.

Maybe, just maybe, Rhys Collins needed a little push in the right direction and she would be the one to help him face his fears. It would all work out in the end....right?

Chapter Eighteen

Rhys

Rhys was just about ready to shoot himself right in his skull to numb the tension headache that had been pounding in his head all afternoon and had gotten progressively worse since Declan and Andi walked in the door. Everyone was having a good time, singing, and dancing, and drinking, and he just wanted to fuck off home and leave them too it.

Thank fuck for small mercy's that Andi and Declan didn't decide to duet yet.

It helped having Shay sitting beside him, and Rhys was aware of the heat of her body next to his, the way her shoulder nudged his whenever Declan or Andi got up to sing or whenever he felt Declan's eyes on him. It normally was super overwhelming for him, being one of the only members of the band that was now alone and having Shay with him, even if they weren't together, made a big difference.

"Hey, you doing okay?" Shay asked him quietly.

"Just ready to get out of here. This shit isn't as bearably when I'm stone cold sober."

Shay brushed strands of her dark hair out of her eyes and Rhys' fingers itched to brush along to silken strands. "I mean, we could leave." She started, glancing around the room. "Or you could get on that stage and shut them all up."

Rhys was already shaking his head before Shay had finished her sentence. "Nope. Not gonna happen. I'd probably make a fool of myself and unless you already told Cathal that you wanted to apprentice, you've got no leverage."

Truth be told, he had considered it...walking up to the stage, sitting down behind the piano and opening his mouth. It would floor Declan, that's for sure and maybe he'd stop glaring at Rhys every five minutes.

"What are you two whispering about over there?" Sinéad, Jameson's girlfriend and Shay's best friend asked with a smile. "It looks very serious."

Rhys flashed the woman a cheeky grin. "I was asking Shay how the hell a gorgeous woman like you ended up with a troll like Jamie. He's definitely punching."

Sinéad laughed as Jameson rolled his eyes, reaching

round with his long arms to give Rhys a little shove. "Hey, don't you be trying to charm her. She's immune to the Rhys Collins seduction."

Flashing Jameson a light-hearted grin, Rhys shrugged his shoulders. "No one is fully immune, man. Besides, what is it that Taylor Swift says...I go on too many dates but I can't make 'em stay."

Jameson barked out a laugh, with both Sinéad and Shay rolling their eyes as Jameson asked. "Since when have you been delving into the wisdom of Taylor Swift, Rhys?"

Rhys took a sip of his coke. "The patient in the room next to mine used to play the song all the time. The lyrics stuck in my head."

When pity flooded into Jameson's eyes, Rhys had to look away, unable to see it. how long would it take before people started to forget his mistakes and appreciate that he was just trying to do better? When would things just go back to being normal again?

Rhys pushed off the seat, waving off the look of concern in Shay's eyes as he went to get himself another drink. It would be so easy to just head out to the bar and get Luna's dad to add a something stronger to his drink. Instead, Rhys leaned against the wall and watched as Jameson got up to play his guitar and sing along to the Verve's, *The Drugs Don't Work*.

Rhys admired how easily Jameson adjusted the song to his tone of voice, how he played the guitar with an ease that Rhys had always envied. His friend had always been uncomfortable with the spotlight, but seeing Jameson on the stage now, smiling as he sang, Rhys was happy for him.

If anyone deserved to be happy it was Jameson.

Rhys watched as Andi got up from her seat next to Declan and walk towards him. Andi leaned against the wall beside him, wrapping her arms around her waist. "You okay?"

Although he was sick to death of everyone asking him that, Rhys had made some steps in repairing his relationship with Andi, and he didn't want to thrust them backwards by being standoffish.

"I'm good, Andi. I told ya the other day if I needed help, I'd ask you. I promise I will."

His sister smiled and bopped his shoulder. "Good. And just a bit of business. I've had a few work things come in and some of them could be good for you. When you feel up to getting back to work, let me know."

Rhys glanced up, his eyes clashing with Declan's before he glanced over at Andi. "I'm not sure I'm even part of the band anymore, Andi."

"Of course you are." Andi tried to reassure him as she lifted her gaze to glare at Declan. "You two are as bull headed as each other. Of you could just have a normal conversation without getting each other's backs up, then maybe ye could resolve some of the issues ye have. And I know I said I wouldn't intervene and I won't, but ugh!!! You two drive me nuts."

Rhys let loose a snort. "Let it go, Andi. You can't fix everything no matter how much of a PR mogul you are. Some things are just broken upon repair and can't be fixed."

Jameson finished his song and they all clapped as he held up his guitar in thanks and Luna bunded up to the stage, a drunken grin on her face. "Okay, mother-fuckers...whose next?"

There was no volunteers, as everyone was content to just chat and enjoy the evening and everyone kinda seemed to ignore Luna, who then whistled and arched her brows high in the air, hands on her hips and Rhys knew Luna would find a victim next, even if she had to drag Noah or Quinn up to sing.

"Rhys will go next."

Rhys snapped his head in Shay's direction so hard it hurt him, his eyes flared as she shifted in her seat as Luna laughed and rolled her eyes. "I'm sure we can find someone to come and perform with Rhys since we all know he sings as well as I do."

"I think he might surprise you." Shay said and Rhys wanted to shake her and scream at her to keep her mouth fucking shut because he wasn't going to make an ass of himself in front of everyone. His body felt it was coiled like a spring, ready to react.

"Rhys."

He dragged his gaze back to look at his sister and when he did, Rhys just knew that Andi knew his secret. He wasn't sure how Andi knew, but she did.

"Maybe it's time for you to be centre stage,"

His heart was racing in his chest and he felt strangely dizzy. Everyone had turned to look at him and he felt like he was under a microscope. Damn Shay and he big mouth. There was no way in hell he was ready to get up there by himself.

Rhys wasn't sure what made him look at Declan, but he did, and when his eyes fell on his best friend, there was a slight curve in his lips that infuriated Rhys, the anger he had been trying to keep under control overflowing to the surface and he just said fuck it.

Perhaps it wasn't the greatest idea to do it because he was seething with anger, pissed off at Shay and definitely pissed off at Declan. Luna must have seen the look on his face because she quickly moved the microphone to the piano and got the hell off the stage.

Rhys shucked off his leather jacket, handed it to Andi, then inhaled a breath before he stalked to the stage and kept his eyes firmly on the piano and the blank wall in front of him. He needed to calm himself down, because the sway of his emotions had his fingers trembling as he sat down in front of the piano.

Swallowing hard, Rhys started to play the first few bars of Green Day's *Boulevard of Broken Dreams*, just to get a feel for the piano, considering he hadn't played it in such a long time. To steady his nerves, Rhys played the entire song in full, trying to figure out what song he wanted, no the song he *needed* to sing.

Lifting his eyes, Rhys looked out at the expectant

crowd gathered, his nerves making butterflies swarm in his stomach. His sister smiled at him encouragingly, at the same time as Declan leaned forward in his seat, leaned his elbows on his knees as if to say to Rhys, come on, show me what you got.

Rhys turned away and closed his eyes, inhaling and exhaling before he forced himself to be calm, telling himself it was just the same as him singing for the patients at the retreat, but deep down he knew that this was so much more than any other performance.

And so Rhys composed himself, fingers hovering over the keys as he prepared to cut himself open and bleed out, and the fear that he wasn't going to be good enough just wasn't as strong as the anger bubbling under his skin.

CHAPTER NINETEEN

Rhys

THE MOMENT RHYS decided to try and wipe the smirk off Declan's face, this eery calmness washed over him and he played the first twenty seconds of intro like he did this every night to millions of people. But that wasn't the truth and the very people he had been hiding from would know all his secrets by the time the song was over.

The song, NF's *Trauma*, was a song Rhys had connected with when he first heard the piano, and the lyrics, and the lyrics themselves were exactly what he wished he could say to Declan. His voice and NF's were sort of similar, not as rock as Declan's or Jameson's but it was a song he could pull off even if the thought of performing in front of his friends and family was nerve-wracking.

Rhys tried to ignore the shocked gasps when he finished the first chorus and played the piano. Then the entire room fell silent as he sang again, his fingers gliding over the keys like they were an extension of his hand. This was where Rhys found his freedom, where he found his courage and he had never, ever felt as brave or as stupid as he did in that moment.

The song was over too quickly, and he extended the end of the song for a few more bars before he lifted his fingers off the keys. He wasn't ready yet to open his eyes and break the spell, crashing him back to reality and to have all of his friends look at him, especially if they hated what they had just heard.

Before he could stop himself, Rhys heard himself call Luna as he started to play the melody for Harry Styles, *Sign of the Times* hoping Luna would get behind her drums to help him as he sang, getting through the first part of the song before he heard Luna on her drums. Rhys sang harder and louder than he had in his life, knowing he needed to belt the lyrics to do the song justice.

He knew he didn't sound too bad, a smile curving his lips as prepared for the higher notes, knowing this was all he had to do to prove himself, to prove he could sing and prove he still had a place in the band, no matter what Declan said or did after tonight. It annoyed him that even after everything, even after all the therapy and all the work he put in, that Declan's opinion still mattered to him. He felt like a teenager again and Declan was the hero who saved him from the bullies.

Rhys finished the song and rose to his feet, only daring to open his eyes so that he could walk to where Luna sat behind her drumkit, mouth hanging open in shock as Rhys held out his fist and bumped her knuckles, not trusting himself to speak.

Keeping his gaze firmly planted on the ground, Rhys felt the weight of his panic against his chest and he needed to get out of there. He headed toward where Andi was holding his jacket, a steady stream of tears falling from her eyes. He vaguely heard Jameson call him, and heard Luna ask him to wait.

He had to stride past Shay to get to Andi, because she had moved to stand beside Cathal some time during his performance. He was fucking pissed as hell at her for making him do this. For forcing his hand and Rhys reacted when Shay reached out to touch his arm.

Jerking his hand away from Shay's touch, Rhys smirked at her before turning to Cathal, who watched Rhys cautiously. "Shay's not happy and you know it. You're so fucking worried about running the shop that you ignore the fact that all she wanted to do is be a tattoo artist. And she lets you get away with it and it's making her fucking miserable. Either offer to train her or let her go to some shop that will let her be her."

Rhys glanced over his shoulder to where Shay had

gone very pale and he shrugged. "A deal's a deal, right? Now we're fucking even."

He hadn't tried to mask the venom in his words and he saw how hurt Shay was and Rhys tried to quash the guilt that surged through him. He wouldn't feel guilty about this...he shouldn't.

Rhys took his jacket from Andi and stormed out into the bar, his blood pounding inside his head as he fumbled in the pocket of his jacket for his keys. When he couldn't find them, Rhys snarled his frustration and kicked the wheel of his car.

"Looking for these?"

Rhys spun at the sound of Declan's voice, saw his friend dangling his keys from his fingers. His face was sombre, a muscle in his jaw twitching like he was trying to keep his features calm and not add to Rhys's anger.

"Andi took them from your jacket," Declan told him, his tone clipped. "She knew you'd run."

"Just gimmie the keys, Dec," Rhys ordered as he took a step toward Declan. "Just gimmie the goddamn keys."

"Not until you tell me what the fuck that was all about? Why the fuck have you lied to me all these years?"

Rhys shook his head, the pounding in his head getting louder. "I don't owe you shit, Declan. I don't owe you or any one else any explanation on how I choose to live my life."

Declan starred at him for the longest time and Rhys contemplated just hitting the road and walking his ass home, rather than stand here and having this argument with Declan that would go nowhere. Rhys heard Declan sigh, then run his free hand through his hair.

"I don't get it, Rhys. I really don't get it."

"What's to get, Dec?" Rhys retorted with a snort. "It is what it is. It was my secret to keep."

Declan took a step toward him and Rhys stood his ground, jerking his chin up, trying to ignore the pain in Declan's eyes.

"I don't get why you felt you needed to keep your voice a secret from your best friend."

Rhys barked out a bitter laugh, with Declan frowning as Rhys tossed his jacket on the bonnet of his car and held his hands out. "Best friend? Is that what you are, Dec? Because if I learned one thing in therapy that lying to yourself is a major part of the problem."

Declan all but growled at Rhys. "What the hell is that supposed to mean? You are my best friend, Rhys. We might be going through some stuff now, but we will get through it."

"Because you need me on side so Andi will marry you."

Declan flinched like Rhys had struck him, and Rhys took that as irrefutable truth that all of his fears from when he was a teen, all his fears that resurfaced when Declan and Andi got together and nothing that

Declan could say now would persuade Rhys otherwise.

Declan scrubbed a hand down his face and shook his head. "How the fuck can you say that? How the hell can you think that?"

Rhys was angered by the hurt in Declan's tone, like Rhys was making this all up in his head, like he was paranoid. Declan had given him all the evidence he needed. Rhys had been diving head first into a pit of despair, and like the lyrics in the song, he had acted out, holding out his hand when he felt like he was drowning and Declan had been so caught up with Andi, that he had simply bypassed it.

Lifting his hand, Rhys rubbed his temple. "Because it's the truth. The moment Andi was back in Ireland, you didn't stop to think how it would affect us, when you went after her. You didn't think about how you hurting my sister would make me see our relationship differently. That it wouldn't change things between us? Jesus, are you that fucking hard-headed? I wish I'd knocked more sense into you at the fundraiser."

Watching as Declan digested what Rhys was trying to tell him, Rhys saw the disbelief on Declan's face and Rhys wondered would Declan ever accept his part in all of this, even if Rhys was willing to accept what he had done to add to the rift. Rhys had spent the last few weeks wondering how he could start to mend all the hurt he'd caused but standing in the cold night air,

Rhys realized that sometimes, what's broken cannot be fixed and it's futile to keep trying.

"Just forget it, Declan." Rhys said with a cold laugh. "I think everyone will be happier if we just park the drama between us for now. I've spent a long time pretending to be something I'm not, someone I'm not. We can just pretend that we hugged it out and you and I are cool. You're off the hook, Dec, I'm giving you an out....you can finally stop pretending to be my friend."

Chapter Twenty

Rhys

"Jesus fucking Christ, Rhys. I was never pretending to be your friend."

"Ya, so it's all in my head, right? Give me a fucking break. But yet again, Declan fucking Walsh can never be in the wrong, right?"

Declan threw his hands in the air. "There is no talking to you when you're like this."

"Like what?" Rhys tossed back at him. "Being honest? Telling you that sometimes I hate myself so much that I drink to forget. Explain how I felt disgusted at myself every time I woke up in some stranger's bed and didn't know where the fuck I was or how I got there? Telling you what's going on in my head and what's been so fucking loud that I decided to try cocaine to block it out?"

Rhys had to work hard to keep his voice from rising and he took a step closer to Declan., huffing out a snort. "It's so fucking funny that I idolized you growing up. I would have done anything for you. Anything. You walked on water, Dec, and I always knew one day I'd know why the fuck you bothered with me. And then I started to see how you looked at Andi and I knew, that was the only reason you became friends with me."

Declan looked like he wanted to protest, however Rhys kept talking. "Was that it? Was I just a means to getting to Andi? Make friends with the idiot brother who couldn't read properly so that she'd like you? You don't have to admit it...I've always known there was no other reason you'd wanna be my friend."

"Rhys," Declan started softly, as if he was afraid of spooking him. "I'm sorry that's what you think but it's not true. Do you know what I thought when Andi finally agreed to give us a shot? That one day, if I was lucky enough to marry her, then you and me would officially be brothers. I swear on my father's life that I didn't use you to get to Andi."

Declan's father had died in a fire a long time ago, leaving Declan to help raise his three siblings with his mam. Rhys truly wanted to believe that Declan wasn't using his dad to try and lie to Rhys, but Rhys felt more confused than ever.

"I saw how you looked at Andi. I knew you liked her. You started spending most weekends at mine and you and Andi started getting closer and closer. It was stupid, but I was jealous. Andi had lots of friends. She was smart and talented and I only had you. You want me to be honest so here I am."

Declan opened his mouth as if to response, the closed it again, his eyes wide.

"I was afraid I was in love with you for years," Rhys said out loud for the first time, even though he had scoffed when his therapist had asked him outright if he was in love with Declan and was angry that he could never reciprocate. "Because I was so jealous. I'm not, yano. So don't freak out. I just think you need to know how you being with Andi has affected me and then I'll leave."

His friend's eyes went wider, and Rhys ran his hand threw his hair and laughed. "I know my feelings are weird. Believe me. But when I'm stressed with the band and need to vent, I could always go to Andi and curse you out for being a control freak and then take the time to realize you were right. I just needed someone to vent to. When something happened at home with the folks or if I had an argument with Andi over stupid shit, I could vent to you and that would be it."

Releasing a sigh, Rhys continued. "And now, I have no one to talk to because if I do, Andi would be forced to keep it from you or worse, fight with you because she's trying to protect me. It's like I've lost the two people in the world I could talk to and it fucking hurts, Dec."

"Okay," Declan said after the longest time, shoving his hands into his jeans pocket. "I get it now. but what I don't get it why you kept it from us the fact that you can sing like that?"

"What? I have a passable singing voice. Who the fuck cares, Dec?"

"I care, Rhys," Declan told him, clearing his voice like he was trying to get rid of some of the emotion in his words, taking a step toward him. "And that's more than a passable voice. Hell Rhys, you can sing. Why would you lie and say you couldn't. I just don't get it."

Rhys felt exhausted, just utterly drained and he was already done with tonight. He knew he sounded tired as he tried to answer Declan. "Because I would never be as good as you. Or Andi. Hell, Andi is so much better than me even on the piano. I knew that being compared to you and her would make me even more miserable. So I just stopped. Have you ever even felt what it's like to be surrounded by all these talented people and just feel like you are the weakest link? Because that's me...every goddamn day."

Lifting his eyes up, Rhys knew Declan was absorbing his words, saw them sink in. Rhys was just about ready to snatch the keys right out of Declan's grasp and bolt. The pain in his head grew and grew, and the ache in his chest had not subsided as much as

Rhys had hoped it would when all of his secrets were laid bare for everyone to see an judge.

Instead, Rhys felt like being up front about how he was feeling had only made the rift between him and Declan even bigger.

"You're not the weak link, Rhys. You never were. And I am sorry if I made you feel like that. You don't have to compare yourself to anyone else. We are all equal in the band. You've got to believe that or else how the hell can we fix this thing between us? I don't want to have to choose between my best friend and the woman I love. C'mon, Rhys, just tell me what you want and we can do it."

Rhys shook his head. "That's it, Dec. I dunno what I want. But right now, I want to go home. So, can you give me my keys so I can get the hell out of here."

"Can we not just sort this out tonight?" Declan asked him, even as he handed Rhys his keys. "I miss my friend."

"And I miss mine, Dec...but answer me one question and if you can answer it honestly, then maybe we can do what you want," Rhys knew he was probably being a bastard by putting Declan on the spot, but it was like his bandmate just wasn't getting the full picture of what Rhys was trying to prove. "If you can promise me that the stuff I shared will be kept between us, that you won't go home with my sister and spill all my fucking secrets to her, then ya, I'll stay and sort shit out. So you tell me Dec, was I right and you being with

Andi has changed us or can you hold off on the pillow talk?"

Rhys mightn't be the smartest man in the world but even he could figure out from the bitch slapped look on his friends face that Rhys had been right and Rhys felt his shoulders slump as he smirked. "That's exactly what I thought. And you don't have to worry about choosing, Dec. it's obvious to everyone you've already chosen Andi."

"That's not fucking fair, Rhys, and you fucking know it." Declan growled, a storm brewing in his eyes.

"Ya, I agree, Dec.. It's not fucking fair. But it is what it is."

Rhys turned away from Declan, headed for the driver's door and opened it, getting ready to get in when Declan grabbed the door, holding it open. "Dammit, Rhys. This isn't over. We need to talk about it some more. I feel like I'm being pulled in two different directions and it's killing me. C'mon man, don't do this."

Declan's voice cracked and Rhys felt his heart lurch. He really wanted to tell Declan that they could work it out, that everything would be okay, but Rhys couldn't put himself in a position where he went back to old habits to make himself forget.

Rhys had always considered that breaking the habits he had meant separating himself from his old party crew and getting his head right, but maybe, all along, the problem hadn't been Rhys coping mechanisms, but the people that made him want to lean on alcohol and sex to not feel.

Maybe, just maybe, in order to heal, Rhys had to cut the ties that hurt him, even for a little while so he could feel well again.

"I'll make it easy for ya, Dec. I'm out. I quit. Find yourself another keyboard player. I can't do this anymore."

CHAPTER TWENTY-ONE

Shay

RHYS HAD IGNORED ALL of her texts and calls since the shitshow last weekend and Shay would never have even given him the push if she thought that things would go down the way that they had, with Rhys telling Declan he was leaving Heartache Melody and to find a new keyboard player. Sinéad had told Shay when she showed Shay around her and Jameson's next place, the couple having decided to move in together.

"Everyone's in complete shock. Jameson isn't sleeping and now that Rhys isn't answering anyone, not even Andi, it's a complete circus. They have to go into the studio to do some additional work for the album but Declan has told Jameson and Luna that unless Rhys changes his mind, he doesn't have the heart to continue with the band that Rhys helped found.

Shay felt like she was responsible for Rhys gut reaction and if he would just speak to her, she could apologize and try and get him to see sense. She was worried he would do something even more stupid and put a halt to his progress.

Cathal had asked her to come to Rebel Ink early this morning and to come up to the newly refurbished apartment upstairs. Shay climbed the stairs that lead to Cathal's apartment, knocking on the door before she opened it with her key.

Walking into the apartment, Shay was confused to see that not many changes had been made to Cathal's existing room, and she called out her friend's name. Cathal emerged from his bedroom, a strange expression on his face and Shay's stomach flipped.

They hadn't discussed what Rhys had said to Cathal, but Cathal had asked her if what Rhys said was true, and Shay had just nodded, before Declan had stalked after Rhys, and Luna had come up to Cathal, halting the conversation.

Today was the first day that Shay and Cathal would be alone and she guessed he would want to clear the air.

Cathal smiled at her then, raising a brow. "Why do you look like you think I'm about to fire you?"

"Aren't you?" Shay asked and Cathal rolled his eyes.

"Rhys was right when he said I didn't want to lose you at the shop. I have been selfish about a few things and I thought you'd speak up if you weren't happy. So I dropped the ball on that, Shay, and I'm sorry."

Shay was already shaking her head. "No, it was me. I love what I do but I should have made it clear that I wanted to apprentice. I was afraid I wouldn't be good and then you'd have to tell me I was shite."

Cathal chuckled softly, folding his arms across his chest. "We are both as bad as each other. it's why we gel so well." He let loose a sigh before continuing. "But first things first. I want to show you something."

Shay followed after Cathal as he walked down the hall, unlocked a door and stepped inside, holding it open for Shay. Beyond the door was another smaller apartment, with it's one entrance and kitchen. It had blank walls and no furniture and was easily bigger than her own hovel.

Confused Shay turned round and looked at Cathal. "Did you decide to rent it out? Or do you plan to have one of the new artists move in?"

Cathal leaned against the kitchen counter, and looked Shay dead in the eyes. "I want you to move in. You'll have your privacy and the joining doors lock, but this place is yours, if you want it."

Shay was shaking her head. "I can't afford a nice place like this, Cathal."

"You can afford it, Shay. It's free." Shay must have looked shocked because Cathal laughed. "You can actually thank Luna because it was her idea. I told her I didn't need all the space and the builders said there was enough space for another apartment, then Luna said that I should just let you move in instead of paying rent on the shithole you were renting."

"But you could make money renting the place out, Cathal."

"Money doesn't matter, Shay. I'm looking out for my sister."

Shay really didn't know what to say, because the money she saved on rent would really help if she did want to apprentice. But how could she even consider leaving when Cathal was being so generous. Her vision blurred, tears threatening to spill out but Cathal shook his head.

"Hey none of that. It's yours, if you want it. You can do whatever you want to the place. I left it blank so you could make it your own. Now...come with me."

Shay followed mutely after her friend, her brain addled as Cathal locked the door to the apartment, handed the keys to her, then showed her how the two apartments were separated. The original staircase that led down to the shop was now between the two apartments, and Cathal went down, leading her into the shop.

Cathal bypassed his new larger room, then past Isaacs and Darren's, to one of the new additional rooms, heading in and Shay was as confused as ever. Inside the room, the area had been already cleaned down and set up, with two chairs and an arm rest put into position. A tray with ink and what looked like a brand new tattoo pen.

"What's all this? You tattooing me?"

Cathal grinned, chuckling softly. "No, dumbass. You're gonna tattoo me."

"No I'm not."

"Ya," Cathal said as he sat down on the chair and placed his arm on the arm rest. "You are. If you wanna be an artist, then you gotta get some practice in. Shay, you already know how to set up a tattoo machine. You know all about hygiene and care. You've watched us long enough to be able to skip all the grunt shit we had to do. You get to tattoo me first. Then Darren and Isaac...Isaac and Darren flipped for who would be second. They fought all day about who got to go next."

"Probably didn't want to be tattooed by a fucking novice." Shay muttered as she sat down on the chair in front of Cathal, slumping in the chair and frowned.

"Shay, the idiots were pissed because they were wanted to get tattooed by you. Darren was thrilled to win the coin toss. Dumbass tried to make me toss for who you got to tattoo first but I told him I'm the boss and it's got to be me."

Shay laughed, rolling her eyes, relief washing over her as she looked at the small patch of space on Cathal's arm, then down at the tattoo machine on the tray beside her. "I don't even have my own machine,

Cathal. And who the hell is gonna run the shop if I'm apprenticing?"

Cathal pulled back his arm and leaned back in the chair. "You will still run the shop but until we can get someone in to help out with just the day to day stuff, like answering the phone, greeting clients and all that, both the lads said they would space out appointments so they can do that while you get in your grove."

Then Cathal flashed her a grin, and there was no mistaking the pride in his voice. "When Barry decided I was ready to tattoo, he gave me my first tattoo machine, did the same for Isaac and Darren and now, I'm continuing the tradition. That machine is yours. A gift from me. I've had the bloody thing for months in case you came to me and said you wanted to give it a go."

Shay didn't know what to say to Cathal, tears leaking from her eyes. She launched herself at him, embracing Cathal as he laughed, and patted her back. When Shay finally let him go, she swiped at her eyes.

"I thought you were going to fire me or tell me that I couldn't apprentice." She admitted, causing Cathal to roll his eyes at her.

"Jesus, Shay... how could I fire you and leave me to deal with Isaac and Darren all by myself."

They both laughed and Shay grinned, excitement making her feel all light and fuzzy.

"So," Cathal broached, motioned upwards with his head. "You gonna move in upstairs?"

"Are you sure?" she asked and Cathal nodded, telling her it made sense, they would make enough money downstairs for her to live rent free upstairs. She just had to pay the bills.

This was more than Shay could have ever asked for, and despite the fact she regretted how the truth had come out, Shay was happier now that everything was out in the open. Now, if only she could get Rhys to answer her and they could talk...then everything would be epic.

"Now that's settled, let's start day one of your apprenticeship. You think you're up for inking me?"

Shay picked up the tattoo pen and turned it on, the buzz sound making her grin as she lifted her gaze to Cathal's before replying. "Fuck ya. Let's do this."

CHAPTER TWENTY-TWO

Rhys

AFTER DROPPING the bombshell that he wanted out of the band, Rhys had managed to shock Declan so hard that he'd let go of Rhys' car door and that had given him the chance to close it and drive away, leaving Declan standing in the car park.

News must have travelled fast, because Rhys had barely driven down the road before his phone started to blow up, with everyone from Shay, to Luna, and Jameson calling him. Andi kept ringing for the rest of the night until Rhys just turned his phone off.

Before he did that, he sent out a group text to whoever might decide to check up on him that he was taking some time to clear his head and no, hat didn't mean he was going on a bender. He had left his phone off for at least forty eight hours and when he turned it back on, he just ignored the million texts and emails, but he did respond to his mam to tell her he just needed to be alone right now. He'd included Shay in the text as well, just in case she decided to show up and have it out with him.

Rhys had used the time to make some decisions. He'd spent a lot of time considering what was best for him, what would make him happy, and then it had hit him; he needed to leave Ireland and carve a new path for himself, away from the ties that bound him.

He'd given his landlord notice of his intent to leave and had even sourced where he could store his things in case he ever came back. Rhys wasn't sure where he was headed just yet, which should have made him more anxious than he was but it had instead made him feel more relaxed and at ease with his decision.

While Rhys was sorting his things, a knock sounded on his door early in the morning and Rhys had gone out to answer it, assuming it was the post or something but Rhys opened the door to see Jameson standing there, a stern expression on his face.

"I need you to come with me." Jameson told him, stepping aside so Rhys would do as asked of him.

"Jay, I've got shit to do. And I meant it when I said I was leaving the band." Rhys wanted to be firm with Jameson about that, him leaving the band but would keep his intention to leave Ireland to himself for a little while.

"I'm not interested in that bullshit today, Rhys." Jameson told him, pointing to the car. "I need help moving my shit to my new place and you did tell me you'd help me, so get your skinny ass in the car before I throw you over my shoulder and carry you to the car."

Rhys had promised Jameson he would help move him move into his new place, the little bungalow that he was moving into with Sinéad. It was the couple's first step into cementing their future together. He knew it was a massive step for Jameson after the loss of his girlfriend when he was a teenager, and Rhys was happy that his friend had been able to find someone like Sinead, who didn't try to erase Layla from Jameson's life, and understood Jameson.

Knowing that he couldn't let Jameson down, Rhys went to grab a jacket, the cold winter months still clinging to Ireland even though spring was just around the corner. He made sure to take his keys and was ready to head out the door when he stopped and looked at Jameson.

"This isn't some weird intervention, right? I'm not gonna rock up to your new gaff and Declan's gonna be there trying to hug it out and get me back in the band?"

Jameson rolled his eyes. "For fuck sake, Rhys. No...I promise there's no one else at the house yet so I promise you're safe. Stop stalling and get in the goddamn car."

Without waiting for Rhys to respond, Jameson stalked to his car and got in, beeping the horn when Rhys made no attempt to follow him. Rhys gave up on resisting and went to the car. They drove in relative silence, with Jameson inserting the odd sentence into the silence during the car trip and once Rhys was sure that any conversation about the band was being avoided, Rhys started to relax.

They slogged it out for most of the day, bringing furniture into rooms and boxes too. There was no unpacking, because Sinéad wanted to help with that, so Rhys just did what he was told. After they had most of the stuff unloaded in their specific rooms, Jameson went to the kitchen and brought back two bottles of Coke and flopped down on the couch.

Rhys eased himself down onto one of the fireside chairs and closed his eyes. He wasn't all that tired but his muscles did ache from all the lifting and pulling. He might like to run now, but that still didn't mean he was used to manual labour...probably something he would have to change when he immigrated.

"I'm sorry, Rhys."

Jameson spoke the words so quietly that Rhys thought he had imagined them, but when Rhys opened his eyes, it was to see Jameson leaning forward in his seat, eyes fixed on him.

"It's all good, Jay. Hot shower and early night and I'll be all set tomorrow."

Shaking his head, Jameson said. "Not about today, Rhys. I'm sorry that I got so wrapped up in my own stuff, with Sinéad and the trial that I just stopped being there for you. I left you to put yourself in situations alone and I'm so fucking sorry for that."

"Listen, Jay," Rhys started, not understanding why the hell Jameson would blame himself for Rhys actions. "The decisions I made, they were my own mistakes, not yours. None of this is your fault and I'm not even sure you could have stopped me. I was set on self destruct mode. I'd never blame you for what I've done. You've got nothing to be sorry for."

"Jesus, Rhys, this whole situation sucks. I know I said I wouldn't bring it up but c'mon man, there is no Heartache Melody without you."

Rhys scratched at the stubble on his jawline. "It's done, Jay. I really wish it hadn't come to this but it is what it is. You guys will be fine without me."

"Declan told us there is no Heartache Melody without you."

Rhys offered Jameson a ghost of a smile. "You know Dec. He thinks saying that will make me feel all important and shit and come running back. He would never let the band die, not even because of me."

Jameson was frowning as he replied. "I think you're wrong, Rhys. I don't think you realise how much Declan cares about you. About us. I'd never seen

Declan cry you know, before you went through that window, but he cried when we arrived in the hospital and he saw that shard of glass in your stomach."

Jesus, Jameson was hitting Rhys where it hurt. Rhys knew the last time Declan had cried was when his dad died, when Rhys had pulled him aside and told him to just let it all out and Declan had cried for his dad and then dried his eyes and had been the strength his mother needed.

Rhys had been unconscious when he arrived in the hospital, and hadn't known who was there until he had woken up after the surgery to remove the glass. By then Declan had been the epitome of calm and Rhys had only to deal with Andi getting emotional with him.

"You also need to talk to Shay, Rhys. Sinéad said she's in bits over what happened. She cares about you too."

Ya, Rhys cared about Shay too...but he had been so angry at her for doing what she did and now, now that he was leaving, what happened really didn't matter. It's not like they could ever be together...

"I'm leaving," Rhys blurted out, watched as Jameson's eyes widened. Rhys had wanted to keep his plans a secret until he told his parents and Andi, however, Jameson needed to know that there wasn't a road back to how it was before. "I gave up the lease of my place. I'm getting out of Ireland."

"Rhys, c'mon," Jameson pleaded, looking shocked

at Rhys revelation. "You can't be serious. You can't just do a runner and leave us all here to deal with the fallout. Think about it, mate. If you go now, then this thing between you and Dec will fester until you two are greeting each other with fake politeness at family gatherings. This isn't the way forward. Promise me you'll reconsider."

Rhys didn't respond to Jameson, knew that the moment he left today that Jameson would be on the phone and telling the band of his plans. Maybe he was better off ripping off the plaster. He would get Jameson to drop him off at his parents' house and tell them tonight, get it over and done with. It would be easier all round.

An unease settled in the pit of his stomach, but Rhys told himself it was just nerves and he was doing the right thing, for him and for the band...

Wasn't he?

CHAPTER TWENTY-THREE

Shay

TWO WEEKS HAD PASSED and still no word from Rhys, and Shay decided she had spent too much time trying to contact him. Besides, the last fortnight had been insanely busy. She had moved out of her apartment and into the one above the shop. She had not only tattooed Cathal, but Darren too, and she was gonna get to tattoo Isaac as soon as the interviews for new artists were through.

Cathal was being his finicky self, the artists that hadn't made the cut far outnumbered the ones that went in the maybe pile. When Shay told him he was being too picky, Cathal had told her that the right people had to feel like family, had to feel like they could all work together with no egos, because none of them were bigger than Rebel Ink.

They were also trying to hire an assistant shop manager to help Shay out but it was hard to find someone who could work part-time. And since they had to work closely with Shay, it was up to her to decide on who she wanted. A lot of the candidates wanted to get their foot in the door in the hopes of apprenticing and while Cathal was looking to get some apprentices in soon, he wanted established artists and Shay wanted someone who wanted to manage the shop and not leave them high and dry should they decide to go apprentice elsewhere.

She really liked this one kid, who looked like she was barely out of school and only wanted part-time hours because she had to look after her little brother. She had almost looked relieved when Shay had mentioned that one of the tattoo artists often brought their daughter to the shop and there would be no problem with her doing that if she needed to.

When Shay had asked her if she wanted to tattoo, the girl laughed and said she couldn't draw a straight line but she was organized and reliable, that raising her brother had meant she had become very time aware and efficient. So Shay had asked her to come by on Saturday morning and bring her brother with her and they would see how she handled herself.

Cathal had approved of Shay's choice, even saying it would be nice for MJ to have a friend around the shop to hang out with. Shay had a good feeling about her, so hopefully, the stars aligned and she worked out.

Shay had been in the back arranging interviews for the next couple of days, working around Cathal's schedule and her own, then worked on the rota a little with her headphones on. Listening to her music helped to keep her focused on her tasks and not go back to worrying about Rhys. It just didn't help when the songs changed and a Heartache Melody song came on, sending her back to looking at her phone.

Seeing that it was after three, Shay got up to see if Isaac had arrived with MJ, the little girl normally coming to say hi when she arrived at the store. Taking off her headphones, Shay heard the steady thump of music from Isaac's room, as he prepped for his afternoon client, and Shay wondered if MJ was ill or had a playdate.

Striding out to the front, she heard the little girl's voice, smiled at the sound of it and then she heard a deep chuckle that stopped her head in her tracks.

"I think you should learn to play the piano too. I'll make sure Luna lets you practice on the one you played when you came to visit last time. Learn to play all the instruments so you can do it all."

"Luna said I could get my own drumkit if I practiced really hard. But I don't think a piano like yours would fit in my nana's house." MJ told him, and Rhys laughed again, sending shivers along Shay's skin.

"That's why I keep my piano at Declan's. But I

think you might be like your dad and get into tattoos. that looks awesome."

Shay stepped out and finally laid eyes on MJ and a clean-shaven Rhys, who was presently being drawn on with a very permanent sharpie marker. Rhys had taken off his jacket and rolled up his sleeve as Melody drew skulls and flowers on his arm, her face scrunched up in concentration.

Ducking under the counter, Rhys lifted his head and smiled at her, and Shay felt like she was a love-struck teenager all over again. Rhys nodded his head at something Melody said, paying full attention to the little girl. Shay grinned when MJ put the lid back on her black marker, then tucked it behind her ear like her dad tended to do, then took out a bright green one and coloured in the skulls she had drawn.

"Hey MJ," Shay said, as MJ lifted her head and smiled.

"Auntie Shay, Rhys said I could practice on him so I can tattoo him when I'm older."

The excitement in her tone said more about the fact that Rhys was in one of her favourite bands and that she didn't realize just how bizarre it was that they were all rubbing shoulders with rockstars because of Cathal and Luna.

MJ went back to her sharpie tattoo as Rhys lifted his head and his full lips curved into a smile as Shay came closer.

"You do realize that's not gonna come off easy,

right?" Shay told him and Rhys winked, making her heart stutter.

"That's cool since I wanna keep it." He replied, his amber eyes dancing with mischief. "I'll just have to skip showers and buy some strong deodorant. Could get pretty smelly though since I'm a boy."

Melody scrunched up her nose, lifted her head, and looked at Rhys. "Daddy says personal hygiene is important. It's okay if you have to wash it off. I can always draw you something new the next time. I don't think people would like you if you were smelly."

Shay had to turn away so she wouldn't laugh out loud, and Rhys himself had to smother a laugh with a cough. MJ continued on with her masterpiece, then declared she was hungry, pushing off her chair as she started to head back to the kitchen, pausing to ask Rhys if he wanted a snack.

"I'm good, MJ. But thank you. Come here for a second."

MJ walked back to where Rhys was still sat, the rockstar taking a twenty out of his pocket and handing it to Melody, who declined it at the start, saying he didn't need to pay her yet. But Rhys just shook his head and pressed the money into the little girl's hand.

"If I was on the street playing music, you'd ask your dad to tip me. You did some awesome art and even if I have to wash it off so I'm not smelly, then you deserve a tip. You can save it towards your piano." Rhys told her with a wink.

Melody grinned then leaned in and sniffed Rhys. "You smell okay to me." Then she walked under the counter, but not before she stopped and looked up at Shay. "Tell Rhys he doesn't smell bad so he won't be sad."

Rhys barked out a laugh as Shay's face reddened at the innocent phrase from the child as Rhys slowly got to his feet. "So, you gonna have a sniff too?"

Shay rolled her eyes, leaning against the counter for support. "Like you need that kind of encouragement." Rhys grinned as he leaned on the counter, and Shay heard herself saying. "You were brill with MJ. That was unexpected."

Rhys laughed again, the sound so melodic it was like a caress on her skin. "I think it's 'cause I'm just a big kid myself. Plus, MJ's not like other kids. She's got this confidence I admire, even if she's like what, seven?"

Shay returned Rhys' smile, then she remembered it had been nearly two weeks since they had spoken and there was so much unsaid between them. She wasn't sure what he was doing here, even if she was glad to see him and despite the fact that things weren't resolved between them, or even with his bandmates, Rhys looked happy.

"Why are you here, Rhys?" Shay asked, curious to know exactly what the rockstar was doing at the shop today. "Finally decided to let one of the lads tattoo you? Although I think you may need to wait for MJ now."

Rhys' expression darkened as he took a step toward her. "I told ya, Shay, if anyone gets to pop my tattoo virgin cherry, it's you. Until then, I came to talk to you. You got time to take a walk with me?"

There was this hungry look in Rhys's amber eyes that made Shay swallow hard, and take an involuntary step backwards, and that action only made Rhys grin even more as she blinked away from the eye contact and went to tell Cathal she was taking a break.

It was just a walk...it doesn't mean a thing...right?

CHAPTER TWENTY-FOUR

Rhys

IT BECAME clear to Rhys that Shay didn't know about his plans to leave Ireland when she didn't chew him out there and then, the moment she laid eyes on him. It had been bad enough telling his mam, who burst out crying the moment Rhys told her of his intentions to leave, his dad not saying much, just going to stick the kettle on. But despite his mam's tears, it wasn't as bad as Andi's reaction.

Jesus, he'd never seen her so mad, her entire face going red with rage as she told him he was stupid, and selfish, called him an idiot, and told him that he was in fucking breach of contract if he didn't finish the album with the band, to which Rhys had replied that he had recorded all his pieces for the album and it was Declan who wanted to go back in and rerecord stuff.

Andi had glared at him, to which Rhys had simply glared back before her eyes filled with tears and she said, "You put us back in each other's orbit, Rhys. You did that and I don't know how it came to this. How did it come to this?"

Rhys had been surprised because he totally thought that Declan would go and tell Andi about his and Declan's conversation and it surprised him into thinking that maybe Declan had taken on board what Rhys had told him.

And then there was Shay...

Once Rhys had taken the time to think over the night at the Sullivan bar, he knew that there had been nothing malicious about what Shay had done and she really was just trying to help him., whereas Rhys had reacted purely out of anger, wanting to hurt Shay in that moment the way he was hurting.

So Rhys had a lot to apologize for before he left Ireland behind, with no destination in mind. His decision was made, right? Then why did it give him a pain in his stomach when he thought of leaving Shay behind.

Was it totally insane that he was tempted to ask her to go with him?

They had been walking for some time, Rhys lost in his thoughts as Shay kept glancing at him, her brown eyes seemed nervous. Her lips were pressed in a firm line, painted a dark gold colour that made her eyes seem bigger, and made Rhys want to drag her into a dark alley and smudge her lipstick.

"So, you wanted to talk?" Shay broached, side-stepping an old woman who came barrelling down the street, glanced at Shay with all her tattoos and piercings, and tutted. Shay ignored the woman, her focus on him and him alone, and to be honest, Rhys liked it.

It was different with Shay than any of the one-night stands he'd had over the last year or two, there was more of a connection, one that thrilled and terrified him.

"Ya," He started, shoving his hands into the pocket of his jeans. "I wanted to say sorry for being an asshole after what went down at the bar, and I'm sorry for giving you the cold shoulder since then. I was being a dickhead and you don't deserve that."

Shay kicked at a stone on the ground sending it skuttling forward. "I shouldn't have pushed you. At the time, I thought it was exactly what you needed, a little nudge in the right direction. I never meant to shove you off the cliff entirely."

Rhys chuckled with a smirk. "I don't think you'd throw me off the cliff, Shay. You think I'm too pretty and that would be a waste." Rhys enjoyed the faint tinge of red that darkened Shay's cheeks and he had to admit, he was having fun flirting with her. "I'm sorry for telling Cathal. I was mad at Declan, not you and I used it to make myself feel better. Didn't work. Only made me feel worse in the end."

Sweeping one of her braids off her shoulder, Shay ignored his flirtatious comment. "How about we just call it even and just go back to being friends? Besides, it all worked out for me in the end. I've moved into the apartment next to Cathal's and I'm gonna apprentice part-time."

"That's awesome, Shay."

Shay grinned, her happiness evident because her smile lit up her face. "I've tattooed Cathal and Darren already so it's defo a start." She worried at her bottom lip, "so maybe if it all worked out for me, then it could work out for you too."

They were headed back the way they had come, so Shay could get back to work, but Rhys stopped walking and leaned against the wall, taking a minute to process his thoughts before he said. "I've left the band."

Shay's mouth gaped open and her eyes went wide. "Shut up. You haven't."

She said it loud enough to make people glance in their direction, so Rhys grabbed her hand, pulled her into the little park, and tried to ignore just how nice her hand felt in his.

"I told Declan that I was. Last week I told my parents I was planning on going away."

"Okay," Shay said, nodding. "That's a good idea. Take a few days and come back and rethink the stupid idea that you are leaving Heartache Melody. That's just insane, Rhys."

A strand of Shay's hair slipped free of its braid and Rhys reached out and tucked it behind her ear, ignoring the sudden intake of Shay's breath. "I'm not going away for a few days, Shay. I'm leaving Ireland. Hell knows if I ever come back."

After studying him for a long moment, Shay stepped back out of his touch. "You're serious? You think it's that easy to just walk away? Music is in your blood, Rhys and the band is too. You can't just walk away like it all means shit and if you really think you can, then you're fucking kidding yourself."

Shay spoke the fears that Rhys had out loud, all the little things Rhys told himself didn't matter. He told himself he could be happy, not making music, not being on stage with his family and he could be content. That starting fresh would be best for him. That leaving everyone behind wouldn't matter.

That leaving Shay behind wouldn't matter.

He had considered asking her to go with him as insane as that sounded, but then she had told him about her apprenticeship and new apartment, and how happy that made her...so he couldn't be selfish and tell her he wanted her to go with him, even if he didn't want to be alone.

Even if he had slowly fallen for Shay when he hadn't been looking for her.

Even when he wasn't sure he deserved someone like Shay to be his.

However, Rhys couldn't help himself as he grinned, running his gaze down Shay's body and back up to her face. "You look hot as hell being all bossy and shit. It's a real turn on."

Shay glared at him, her hands falling to her hips. "Don't."

"Don't what, gorgeous?"

"Don't use flirting to try and change the subject. You can't just blurt out that you plan on buying a one-way ticket out of Dodge and then flirt with me like you want to kiss me or something."

Rhys took a step toward Shay, letting the heat he felt in his body show in his eyes. "I do want to kiss you, Shay. I want to touch you so bad that it hurts."

She swallowed hard, angling her head up and it would have been so easy for Rhys to close the distance, to crush his lips to hers and finally taste her like he'd wanted to since the first moment their eyes had clashed across the room. He wanted to feel her gasp as his tongue explored her mouth and feel her body pressed against him, connecting in all the right places.

He was thinking about getting Shay naked and he almost missed it when she replied. "I want you to kiss me too."

Rhys was about to tell her that his ninety days would be up in a few short weeks and then he would kiss her, but Shay took another step back and shook her head. "I want you to kiss me, but not if it means we have to say goodbye. It would be cruel to both of us and we don't deserve that pain. So even though I want you to kiss me, unless you plan on hanging round to see if we could have something. We'll have to just be happy with being friends."

Shay turned around and walked out of the park, leaving Rhys alone, a heaviness in his chest as he watched Shay walk away and realized just how much it hurt him to let her go. It was like a bolt of lightning to the chest, like the ground was shifting beneath his feet as Rhys began to understand exactly what falling in love meant for the first time in his life.

CHAPTER TWENTY-FIVE

Rhys

RHYS HAD MULLED over what Shay had said for a few days and contemplated all of the things he had discovered. Falling in love was not something Rhys ever considered would happen to him, but now that he knew he was falling for Shay, it had offered him some clarity about the things that had often sent him into a spiral.

He'd spent a lot of his life afraid. Afraid that Declan had been pretending to be his friend. Afraid that he wasn't good enough to be part of the band. Afraid he wasn't smart enough. Afraid that everyone around him was moving on with their lives and would one day forget about him and leave him all alone.

Afraid. Afraid. Afraid.

But Rhys was tired of being afraid and he was fucking sick to death of trading his happiness to protect himself from getting hurt. He used to convince himself he was okay with being alone, but that was another goddamn lie. Rhys knew he had spent his entire life mistreating himself because deep down, he felt like this was what he deserved.

After years of being untrue to himself...it had taken a gorgeous tattoo artist to call him on his bull-shit, and the thought of losing her made Rhys consider that it was time for him to fight through his fears, in the hope that his life could be better.

And so today he decided it was time to start making amends for all the pain he had caused. He had already decided that he was staying in Ireland, even if he couldn't get back the lease on his place, and maybe that was for the best...a fresh slate.

Rhys let himself into Declan's place in the afternoon, then keyed in the code for the studio. The moment he entered he heard the unmistakable sound of Declan playing his acoustic guitar. It wasn't a melody that Rhys had heard before but it instantly made him start to hear the piano arrangement that could accompany it, could hear the drumbeat that Luna would kill on. He smiled at how easy Jameson would take the acoustic sound and riff it on his own guitar.

"Rhys."

Andi's voice dragged him from his thoughts and he offered his sister a genuine smile as she watched him warily.

"What are you doing here?"

There was a tightness in her tone, like she was expecting Rhys to cause a scene and Andi was preparing to put herself between her brother and her lover. Rhys looked at his sister, really looked at her, and noticed the weight loss and the tiredness behind her eyes. The only other time he'd seen his sister in such a state was after the gala dinner, when he'd punched Declan.

"I'm not here to cause trouble, Andi." Rhys tried to reassure her, striding into the centre of the room. "I just came to talk to Dec."

Andi glanced over her shoulder, then back at Rhys. "Declan's just working on some stuff. Maybe you could come back later, and we can have dinner and talk."

Rhys smiled, disappointed that Andi really wasn't going to let him speak to Declan, and yet, he didn't blame her at all. It made sense that Andi would not only be protecting the man she loved, but hopefully, she also saw the brother who realized he had been a complete and utter asshole and was ready to try and make amends.

"Sure. That sounds good. I just wanted to let you and him know that I decided to stay in Ireland. Can't keep running from my problems or shit will never get resolved."

Andi's eyes widened and she came forward. "You're staying?"

Rhys shrugged, snorting slightly. "Ya, well, if I can find a new gaff to stay in. Landlord already had someone ready to move into mine and I don't really fancy moving in with the parents. Not really the rockstar look, is it?"

He barely had time to brace himself before Andi lunged forward, engulfing Rhys in a bear hug. Letting loose a sigh, Rhys wrapped his arms around Andi and just held her, trying to ignore the wetness on his tee as Andi cried. He tried to peel her off so he could leave, and she kept her arms wrapped tightly around him.

"Hey, don't cry. I'm sorry I've been a dick. I'm sorry for being so messed up. But you know I love ya, right sis?"

Andi finally let him go, sweeping at her eyes. "I love you too, Rhys."

"Listen, I'll head out and I can meet up with Declan another day. No need to disturb him while he's got something good going. I need to look for a new place anyways."

"Rhys."

Lifting his head to where his best friend stood in the doorway leading to the rehearsal space, from the look on Declan's face, he had witnessed the exchange with Andi, but his lips were pressed into a firm line and apart from almost growling Rhys' name, Declan didn't say anymore.

Andi glanced from Rhys to Declan and back again and Rhys could see her tense as Declan strode toward them, standing beside Andi, his eyes fixed on Rhys.

"I told Rhys you were working on something so he agreed to come back another time and we can all eat together," Andi said as she slipped her fingers into Declan's and then stole a glance at Rhys to see if he would react, and she sighed when Rhys barely spared their intertwined fingers a second glance.

"I heard," Declan answered, bending to kiss Andi on the cheek. "Gimmie a few minutes with Rhys and then we can eat. Why don't you order some Chinese from that place you like? You haven't eaten all day."

Andi hesitated, not bothering to look at Declan, just held Rhys' gaze so Rhys grinned, winking. "Go and order food, Andi. We just have some stuff to talk about before we all eat. I promise to behave."

That seemed to mollify Andi, as she squeezed Declan's hand and walked by Rhys, resting a hand on his arm before she left him alone with Declan. They waited until they heard the door close, locking them inside and nerves started to make his stomach feel queasy.

"So, you're staying?"

"Ya, I am," Rhys said, then he ran a hand through his hair. "Listen, before you say anything else. Let me get some stuff off my chest first before I lose my nerve and fuck it all up."

Declan didn't say anything in response, just inclined his head and Rhys felt the words tumble from his lips in a rush.

"I'm sorry. I'm sorry for being a dickhead to you because I was scared of losing our friendship. I'm sorry for pushing and prodding because I was afraid of losing my sister. I made some shitty choices and really bad decisions, hurting myself because I felt like I deserved it. But I think I understand now, what you and Andi have. I don't think I did before and I was confused. Things will change between us, because of you and Andi, but I hope that once you realize I'm not going to be a fuck up anymore, we can start to work toward being friends again."

Declan stared at him for the longest time before he spoke. "I'm sorry I let it get this far. I didn't see what the issue was until you laid it out for me. I just thought you were being a pain for the sake of it and I was confused too. But you are my best friend Rhys. You are like a brother to me and nothing, nothing you do will ever change that. I was too wrapped up in trying to make sure I didn't fuck things up with Andi, that I fucked them up with you instead."

Rhys shifted his weight from one side to the other. "You think we can start with a clean slate? I'll try and be less dickish."

A rumble of laughter came from Declan. "Man, I've missed you."

Warmth spread through Rhys' chest as he held out his hand, surprised when Declan pulled him in for a hug. "I missed you too, Dec. I missed you too."

They separated, and Rhys was shocked to see a sheen of wetness in Declan's eyes.

"The new song sounded good," Rhys told him as he cleared his throat.

"Saving it for album two. I thought we could work on it together before bringing the others on. And I want you to sing on it with me."

Rhys grinned as he realized that no matter if they weren't talking, Declan had been working on a song that included him, that he wanted him to be a bigger part of and Rhys was thankful that he had decided to stay.

"We can do that. Now, before she comes back to see if we've killed each other, tell me how you plan to propose to my sister."

Declan blinked, obviously surprised that Rhys would bring it up, a look of relief flashing over his features before he grinned and Rhys knew that everything would be all right in the end.

CHAPTER TWENTY-SIX

Rhys

RHYS HADN'T time over the next two weeks to go in search of Shay and any texts he'd sent her had gone unanswered. He wanted her to know that he had decided to stay because of what she had said, but he wanted to do it face-to-face, and not with a text.

Declan had been planning his proposal with Rhys' help, taking up most of his time. He had a couple of weeks before his lease was up, and had arranged some viewings, so that was a start. It was only when he had sat down with Declan yesterday and his friend had remarked on how he couldn't believe it had already been three months since he left the retreat that Rhys had been aware of it.

And while Rhys was thrilled he had managed to see it through with only the one almost slip-up, he was a little conflicted that the crutch of his three-month sobriety was over, and now, it was all up to Rhys to make the decisions on whether he wanted to drink and have sex...and he really wanted to have sex with Shay.

It didn't slip Rhys' mind that they hadn't even kissed yet and it seemed like the most torturous foreplay that Rhys had experienced in his life, and it just made him hungry for more. The thought of getting Shay naked had been at the forefront of his mind since Declan had reminded him that his ninety days were over.

He hadn't been able to settle this evening, pacing the length and breadth of his bedsit, erotic images playing over and over in his mind, and his cock was so hard that it hurt. After tossing and turning in his sleep, Rhys had decided to give in to the madness and drive to Shay's new apartment over the tattoo shop.

All the lights were out as he jogged up the stone steps leading to the side door, as Rhys knocked hard a couple of times, then leaned against the railing as he waited to see if the knocks would rouse Shay from sleep. A light flicked on inside, and Rhys' pulse began to race as the door opened slowly, a very sexy and half-asleep Shay rubbing her eyes.

"Rhys? Is everything okay?"

Shay always had a deeper almost husky tone, but Rhys noted just how devilishly sexy she sounded half asleep. Rhys roamed his eyes over Shay, dressed in nothing more than a tiny pair of shorts and a string top, her tattooed skin on display. Her hair hung loose around her shoulders and Rhys wanted to fist his hand in her hair and drag her in for a kiss that would be his ending.

"Rhys?"

When she repeated his name, shivering slightly at the cold of the night, her nipples hardening before his eyes, Rhys licked his lips, taking a step forward. "It's day ninety-three."

"Huh?" She asked, obviously confused and still not fully awake.

Taking another step toward Shay, forcing her to open the door a little wider, Rhys curved his lips into a smile, Shay blinking as he leaned in and said again. "It's day ninety-three."

Something seemed to register in her head because Shay sucked in a breath and her lips parted slightly, the pink of her tongue flicked out to her bottom lip and something snapped in Rhys. Reaching out, he cupped Shay's face in his hands and crushed his lips to hers before she could protest or do anything.

The moment his lips touched hers, and Shay's moan vibrated against his lips, Rhys was addicted, devouring her mouth, *fucking* her mouth like he was starving, plunging his tongue into her mouth, and lapping at her tongue. His hands made their way down from her face, blazing a trail down her body until they cupped the firmness of her ass and started to walk them inside the apartment.

Rhys kept kissing her, his chest burning with the need to take in air, and yet, he had never felt so alive, Shay's hands sliding up his chest and when she gave him a gentle but firm push, Rhys pulled back, giving Shay just a little space.

Shay backed against the wall, closing the door with a trembling hand and Rhys backed up to the other wall. Her lips were red and kiss swollen, her breathing ragged, her palms now flat on the wall like she didn't trust herself to not reach for him.

There was nothing but a step between them in the narrow hallway, Rhys far too warm in his leather jacket. He stripped it off, dropped it where he stood, as Shay watched him, a lust in her eyes that mirrored his own.

"You can't...," Shay started to say, swallowing hard like it was hard for her to speak, that sensuous low tone doing nothing to quench the thirst in Rhys. "You can't just show up at my house at the ass crack of morning and kiss me like that. Not now. I don't care if your ninety days are up or not, Rhys. I meant what I said. You can't kiss me like that when you plan on leaving."

"I'm not."

"Sorry...what?"

"I'm not leaving. I'm staying. Now can I go back to kissing you?" Rhys teased, taking a step closer, stopping when Shay placed her hands on his stomach. He could still have lowered his head to kiss her, but instead he leaned his forehead against hers and sighed. "You're killing me, babe. My cock had been hard since the first time I saw you across the bar, before I knew who you were."

Shay's eyes widened, her hands starting to travel up toward his chest and then Rhys heard her say. "Fuck it."

Her fingers grasped his tee and yanked him to her, their lips colliding once more as Rhys pressed into her, grinding his hard-on against her as he went back to fucking her with his mouth. Rhys wanted to spend time tasting and teasing her body, but he knew that if he did that, he might not last very long and he just wanted to be inside her, even if it meant taking her up against the wall.

Breaking the kiss, Rhys trailed his lips down her neck, making his way to her perfect handfuls of breasts, cupping one roughly with his hand and lowered his mouth to suck the other through the cotton of her top. Shay groaned, her hands going to his hair, and she curved a leg around his waist, bringing her centre in line with his raging hard-on.

Rhys slid a hand between their bodies, found that Shay's shorts were already wet and Rhys about damn lost his mind. He stopped suckling on her breast long enough to yank her top over her head, then removed his own, then Shay unhooked her leg to slide her shorts down over her ass and kicked them aside, standing before him gloriously naked.

"You are a goddess," Rhys told her, pulling at the belt of his jeans, then stripped them off, was about to give his cock a stroke when Shay reached out and took matters into her own hands. "Fuck, Shay. Stop or I'll come and I really want to be inside you when I do."

A slow, seductive smile crept over Shay's lips. "Then fuck me, Rhys. Right here, right now."

Rhys heard himself growl, bending down to find the condoms he'd brought just in case, making quick work unwrapping and rolling it on. Then Rhys lunged for Shay, kissing her again, and he didn't think he would ever get tired of kissing her.

His mind almost scrambled as he positioned them so that he could start to push his cock into her, Shay's hands wrapping around his neck, his hands cupping her ass as he thrust into her fully in one stroke, her gasp coming out in a heady moan. Her walls clenched around his cock, and he paused to give Shay a second, even though he knew he wasn't going to last much longer.

He wanted her too much and it had been a while.

"Fucking move, Rhys. Move."

She scrapped her nails along his scalp and that was Rhys's undoing, as he lost off finesse and just continued to slide in and out of Shay, her back slapping against the wall and the only sounds made were the expression of their pleasure. Rhys felt Shay tremble in his arms, knew she was close to orgasm, and knew his own release was not far away, lifting his head to lock with Shay's gaze and the moment their eyes clashed, Shay barked out a curse and came hard, the clench of her walls as she orgasmed, sending him over the edge with one final thrust.

Neither of them said anything for a moment, Rhys still inside her, their eyes still locked with one another, both of their chests rising and falling rapidly as they tried to catch their breaths. Then Shay smiled, making Rhys want to kiss her again, so he did just that.

And in that moment, still sheathed inside of Shay, Rhys realized that the feeling in his chest was more than just lust, more than sexual chemistry, and it felt like waking up.

Chapter Twenty-Seven

Shay

Shay woke up the next morning, the sexiest rockstar in her bed. Their frantic sex in the hall had been wild and passionate as hell, and Shay had been woken during the night by Rhys who played her body like he played his keyboard. She was a melted goo of satisfaction when she pried her eyes open this morning.

Rhys was still asleep, curled into her body, one hand resting on the curve of her breast, the other cupping her thigh as she lay on her back. His face was pressed into the curve of her neck, her skin tickling with every exhale of breath as Rhys slept on.

Looking down at Rhys' profile, Shay drank in the peacefulness on his face, and she realized just how much of a front Rhys put on in front of everyone else. His hair was unkept, that sexy I just got out of bed kinda mussed that made Shay want to run her fingers through it. His lips were slightly parted, his sharp angles less so with such a relaxed expression on his face.

His body too seemed relaxed, and Shay had seen Rhys shirtless a number of times on stage, and yet, the clean living over the last few months had filled out his slender frame, lean muscles on a torso that led down to slender hips and a firm ass that made Shay smile.

Shay sucked in a breath as Rhys' hand started towards her core, delving between her folds, and the moan that escaped her lips as she arched into his touch filled the room. Full lips dragged down her throat, then Rhys sucked hard on the curve between her neck and her shoulder.

"How long have you been awake?" Shay managed to grind out as Rhys stroked a finger in and out of her core, the hand near her breast moving to cup her small mounds.

"Enough to see you perving on me," Rhys said with a chortle of laughter. "You were fucking me with your eyes, Shay Gleeson and I liked it."

Shay couldn't answer Rhys because he inserted a second finger, then shifted his body so that he could flick his tongue over her nipple, then suck on her breast. Shay let loose a groan, the pressure in her building and building like the crescendo in a song, the powerful, sure strokes of Rhys' fingers made her clench the sheets with her fingers trying to hold off her release so she could ride the waves a little longer.

Then Rhys stretched her walls by adding a third digit and Shay broke part with a scream of Rhys' name, her body trembling and trembling as Rhys continued to stroke her through the aftershocks of her climax.

When she was finally sane enough to look at him, Shay rolled her eyes at the look of very male satisfaction and the totally erotic way that Rhys licked his fingers, the ones that had been buried deep inside her and were coated in her wetness, like he was licking his favourite lollipop.

"Mmm," The devil moaned as he pulled his fingers out of his mouth with a pop. "I could get used to walking you up in the morning with you coming on my fingers."

Shay shoved him hard, getting a dark chuckle for her effort as Rhys rolled over onto his back and folded his hands across his chest, a stupid grin on his face, the duvet having slipped down to lay across his slim waist, and he did nothing to hide the fact he was aroused.

"Not that I wanna get up but we could head out for breakfast. I promised Declan I'd meet up with him later but until then, I'm all yours."

Shay rolled so that she lay on her side, looking down at Rhys as he reached up and brushed her face from her face with a smile. Shay couldn't stop herself from bending to press a quick kiss to his smiling lips. Shay broke the kiss before she forgot that she and Rhys needed to talk things through before she let herself get too deep.

"I know you said you were staying, but what does that mean for us?" Shay asked, shifting to rest her head on her palm when Rhys frowned.

"Did I not explain myself clearly last night?" Rhys asked and Shay could see the hint of uncertainty in his eyes. "I want to be with you. I know I've never been in a relationship before and I'm not too sure how to be in one, but I want to be with you. And I want everyone to know that we are together."

Shay couldn't not touch him, so she ran her hand through his hair. "I want to be with you too. But Rhys, you're about to finish your album and then there's the tour. I have my apprenticeship."

Rhys' amber eyes darkened as he sat up in the bed and Shay did the same, pulling the sheet up to cover herself because she felt naked enough with this conversation.

"So, what? Cathal and Luna make it work. Sinéad and Jameson make it work. Or is it that you don't trust me to behave when on tour? Or has the fantasy of being with a rockstar not lived up to your expectations?"

Shay knew that Rhys wasn't trying to be hurtful, he was just feeling insecure, and Shay was starting to realise when Rhys felt insecure, he became a master at deflecting.

"That's not what I meant," Shay started, reaching

out so she could rest her hand on Rhys's chest and she felt the way his heart raced like he was scared of losing her. "Long distance is hard with stolen moments here and there. I'm willing to give it a go too. I trust you, Rhys. And I'm not with you because you are a rockstar. I'm with you because you are Rhys and I happen to like Rhys very much."

The lopsided smile that Rhys gave her made her want to kiss him again and she did, shifting so that she straddled his waist, his erection pressed hard against her stomach. The kiss was a slow, claiming kiss, with Rhys letting her set the pace as he sank his fingers into her hair. They licked and tasted and played for a time, until the heat between Shay's legs grew and grew and she needed to have Rhys inside her again.

Rhys obviously had the same idea, because he was already reaching for a condom as Shay wrapped a hand around his thick cock, stroking it and smiling at the guttural groan that fell from Rhys' lips. With her free hand, she plucked the condom packet from his fingers, ripped it open, and sheathed him. Shay lifted off him, placing her core at the head of his cock, and slowly, lowered herself onto him.

They both moaned, this angle giving Shay all the control as she started to ride Rhys, lifting up and easing back down for once, twice, and then Rhys' hands caught her waist, pulling her fully onto him so that he was fully buried inside her.

Rhys lifted his head off the headboard, arching his

hips up as soon as Shay started to move again, their breathing and moans, and the sound of their bodies joining the only music they needed. Shay felt another release coming seconds before she exploded, sinking down onto Rhys as her walls fisted his cock and as she rode the immense waves of pleasure, Rhys flipped them and continued to slide in and out of her, sweat beading on his forehead until he grunted, filling her once more as he came and his release set Shay off again.

Afterwards, once Shay had come back from peeing, and Rhys had discarded the condom, they lay in each others' arms, neither of them wanting to break the spell around them, content to lay in bed, until both their stomachs rumbled and they showered and dressed to eat some food that Shay had in her fridge.

Rhys kissed her hard on the mouth when he had to leave, promising to come back as soon as he could. Shay opened the door and let Rhys leave, closing the door behind her and leaning against it, letting out a sigh.

There was no way Shay was going to be able to keep her and Rhys a secret for long and while it was still shiny and new, who knew when Rhys would want to be public with their relationship? Striding into her sitting room, she picked up her phone from where it had fallen last night and called the one person that would understand what it was like to date a rockstar.

"Sinéad, get your ass over here."

"Shay? You okay?" Her friend asked and Shay laughed as she sank down on her couch.

"I've just had lots of dirty, dirty sex with a rockstar and I need your help to process it."

Shay heard a bark of laughter, then she grinned as Sinéad said. "I'm on the way. I'll bring beer."

CHAPTER TWENTY-EIGHT

Rhys

THE NEXT COUPLE of days flew by in a whirlwind and Rhys had never felt so content in his life. He had his band, his music, his friends, and a gorgeous woman to call his. They hadn't discussed labels or anything, or when they would go public with the fact that they were together, but Rhys wasn't going to hide him and Shay from the rest of the gang; he just needed the right time for everyone to find out.

Tonight was the night that Declan was planning on proposing to Andi, and it was Rhys's job to make sure Andi got to where she needed to be. Rhys had taken her out for dinner, keeping it casual because Declan didn't want his proposal to be for the public, he wanted to make it all about him and Andi, and Rhys was the only person besides his parents that knew it was happening.

Declan had called Rhys maybe a million times to make sure that Rhys knew what he was supposed to do. Rhys told Declan not to stress and that everything would be grand. He had wondered why Declan had asked him to be the one to keep Andi out tonight, but then it dawned on him that if Declan had simply proposed, then she might say no out of fear that it would disrupt the tentative peace between him and Rhys.

It had been tough trying to go back to before, the snark and the angst on the tip of his tongue. But Rhys managed to remind himself that Declan and he had cleared the air and were working on getting their friendship back on track. Declan had invited him over a few times to work on band stuff, asking Rhys to help him with new songs for the second album and trying to convince Rhys that he should sing on the last song they had to record for their debut.

Rhys had told Declan he would think about it, and they had left it at that...until they were due back in the studio to finish the album. And then the release of the album meant a tour and a different city, maybe a different country every other day.

"I'm glad you and Dec seem to be getting along better," Andi said, interrupting his thoughts as she linked her arm through his as they walked back to her and Declan's apartment. There was an air of trepidation in her words like she was trying to suss Rhys out to see if the progress Andi had seen was a true reflection of how things were going.

Rhys ran his free hand through his hair. "Ya, we are. It's going to be okay, Andi. You can stop stressing now. I'm sorry that I caused you so much pain because I was confused and self-destructive."

Andi leaned against him, letting loose a sigh before she replied. "And I'm sorry if I caused you pain too, Rhys. Declan hasn't told me all of what ye spoke of. He said that sometimes, there are things he can't tell me, not because he's keeping stuff from me, but because he has to honour your friendship. So, I told him the same and we agreed we would keep things to ourselves unless it would hurt any of us...the three of us that is. I hope that's okay."

Rhys was surprised to hear that Declan hadn't told Andi everything, and he must have kept the darker side of their conversations to himself because Andi hadn't asked him about Rhys and his confusion about his feelings for Declan. Maybe just maybe, everything would be grand in the end.

They came to a stop outside the studio as Andi reached for her keys, her gaze narrowing in surprise when Rhys pulled her toward the building next door. Rhys grinned, putting a finger to his lips when Andi frowned.

"Close your eyes, Andi."

"What the hell is going on, Rhys?" Andi demanded and Rhys reached out and placed his hands on his sister's shoulders.

"Do you trust me?" He asked, his smile widening as Andi rolled her eyes as if to say well duh, then lowered her lashes. She let Rhys steer her inside the door of the building next door, manoeuvring her in the darkness.

"No peaking now. keep your eyes closed until I tell ya."

"You're not planning on killing me, are you? This definitely has murder room vibes, Rhys."

Rhys chuckled, giving Andi's arm a little squeeze as he opened the door where he knew Declan was waiting and gently nudged Andi inside before he said. "I love you, Andi. Open your eyes."

Before Andi could respond to him, Rhys backed out of the room, leaving the door slightly ajar so he could film the proposal for Andi and Declan to have. He watched as Declan came forward to Andi, wading through roses that were spewed on the floor and candles that were lit all around the room.

"Declan? What's all this? Oh my god, did you and Rhys break into the building next door and do this?" Andi looked around. "Where did Rhys go?"

Declan smiled, but Rhys could see the nerves on his friend's face. Andi was so distracted by the prospect of them having broken into the budling that she failed to notice Declan fidgeting with something in his pocket. Rhys had never seen Declan look so frazzled.

"We didn't break in Andi." Declan said as he reached out and took Andi's hand in his. "This is a present to you, well you and Charlie, from me and Noah. We pitched together and bought the rest of the buildings on this side of the lot. This here, is the new home of Rebel PR, and the building next door to this, will be the gym me and Noah plan on opening that caters to athletes."

Rhys watched as Andi's eyes widened, her lips parting. "How did you manage to keep this from me? From Charlie."

Declan shrugged, a smile curving his lips. "Once me and Noah decided we wanted to make sure you and Charlie were nearby, and the buildings went up for sale, we knew we had to get Charlie onboard and she agreed it was perfect. There's even space over the gym for a loft apartment that we hoped Rhys would move into. If he wants to."

Rhys blinked in surprise, nearly dropping his phone in shock that Declan had factored him into things as Andi flung her arms around Declan's neck. "I can't believe you've done this. I'm gonna kill Charlie for keeping it a secret."

Andi detangled herself from Declan and looked around, starting to point out where they could put offices, where the reception area could be, where would make the perfect conference room, and so on. His sister was so engrossed in her planning that she was oblivious to Declan taking the box out of his pocket and getting down on one knee.

"Andi."

Andi was so excited that it took Declan two more tries of saying her name before she turned round and stopped dead. Her eyes widened, her hand going to her mouth as Declan swallowed hard.

"Andrea Anastasia Josephine Collins, I fell in love with you the first moment that I managed to make you laugh, when you argued with me about music and I never stopped, even when our stubbornness kept us apart. The moment we finally kissed, I knew that there would never be another woman for me. You are my muse and my heart. I know we haven't been a couple for that long, but we spent so much time apart and I never want not to be yours. Andi, I love you...will you marry me?"

Declan remained on the floor, holding up the diamond ring to Andi, who looked at the ring like she was utterly terrified, and Rhys' stomach sank for a moment, wondering if Andi was so scared of commitment that she might just do a runner.

Tears welled in Andi's eyes as she took a step toward Declan, reaching out to cup his cheek as she sucked in some air and then dropped her hand from her mouth, the most dazzling smile on her face. "Yes, Declan. Yes...a thousand times yes. I love you too."

Declan surged from the floor and took Andi in his

arms, but not before he placed the engagement ring on Andi's finger. Rhys smiled, genuinely happy for his sister and his best friend, halting the recording and retreating from the building, and allowing the happy couple their privacy.

Rhys was halfway down the road on the way to his apartment when his phone pinged. He pulled up the picture Declan had sent him, of Andi holding up her ring with the caption, -You fancy being my best man?

Laughing into the night, Rhys smiled at how crazy it was that a mere couple of weeks ago, he would have been sickened at the thought of Andi and Declan getting married, and now, here he was replying that he would be honoured back to Declan and actually meaning it.

Life was funny sometimes, wasn't it?

CHAPTER TWENTY-NINE

Shay

"ARE you sure you wanna make us official here, tonight? I mean it is your sister's engagement party." Shay asked Rhys as they drove up towards the studio and Declan and Andi's home, where the two were hosting a small family and close friends get-together.

Rhys glanced over at Shay, his amber eyes shining in the darkness. "Course it is. Plus it's only the band and the Rebel Racers crew... and Sinéad will be there with Jameson...Cathal will be there with Luna. I want everyone to know that we're a thing."

When Rhys leaned over and kissed Shay on her cheek, she could have swooned. She loved this side of Rhys as much as the playful side of him. It wasn't a side of him that the fans or the public saw very often, used to his bad boy image, and that made Shay feel special because she felt that this was the real Rhys.

Although, she loved his bad boy side too....especially when he was focused on her.

Getting out of the car, Shay fidgeted with her leather jacket, ignoring the amused look from Rhys as he waited for her to be ready. She was feeling a little intimidated, and Shay was not used to feeling intimidated. It was part of her job to be confident and organized but she was super nervous about meeting Rhys's sister Andi for the first time as Rhys' girlfriend.

Girlfriend...even now it sounded strange and when Rhys had introduced her to his parents as his girlfriend last night when she went for dinner, it had given her that schoolgirl kinda feeling. Shay wasn't used to being around parents who were supportive and loving but being around Rhys parents made Shay see exactly how she would want any of her kids raised.

"C'mon, it won't be that bad," Rhys told her as he pulled open the door and held it open for her.

"Such a gentleman." Shay teased him, starting to head up the stairs.

"I just wanted the perfect view of your ass."

Shay laughed, shaking her head as she grinned like an idiot, reaching the top of the stairs and inhaling a breath before she opened it and stepped into the loft apartment.

Heads turned in their direction, making Shay's face

heat, but then Rhys was beside her, a hand on the small of her back as he said. "Well, the party can start now I've arrived."

A chortle of laughter rang out amongst the friends, Rhys nudging her into the room as they made the rounds and said hello to people, Rhys making sure that they ended up by Jameson and Sinéad. Her best friend grinned, handing her a drink and Shay took a big gulp.

"Does this ever get less strange?" Shay asked Sinéad quietly while Rhys chatted to Jameson.

"Rubbing shoulders with rockstars and race car drivers? Nope. Wait until you knock on a door wearing an Oli Scott t-shirt and he opens it. That's when you know you've stepped into the twilight zone."

Shay chuckled, shaking her head, realizing that her semi-normal life would never be the same again, however, if that meant she got to be with Rhys, she would just have to deal with it all. Cathal and Luna came over and the conversation drifted toward Shay and her apprenticeship, then to the new girl that Shay was training up to work in the shop.

Declan called Rhys over and Shay kept an eye on her boyfriend, saw him smile as he embraced Declan and congratulated him again. Shay was relieved that the two had managed to get through the bad times, and Rhys really was genuinely happy for his sister and his best friend.

"It's nice to see someone look at my brother like that."

Shay turned at the sound of the voice, coming face to face with Rhys' sister, Andi. She had similar features to Rhys, in the shape of the eyes and the nose, but Andi's features were less sharp than Rhys. But still there was no denying the family resemblance.

Andi's warm smile deepened as she held out her hand. "I'm Andi. It's nice to properly meet you."

"Shay," she replied stupidly and almost cursed herself. "But you knew that. Congrats by the way, I saw the video Rhys took of the proposal. It looked romantic."

Andi glanced over to where Declan and Rhys were having an animated conversation with Luna, but everyone was smiling. Declan glanced up, winked at his fiancé, and Rhys mock punched him in the shoulder, telling Declan to stop making goo-goo eyes at his sister.

Then Rhys glanced at Shay, a slow, deliberate smile curving his lips, then he let loose a joyous sound of laughter as Declan mimicked his actions and told Rhys to stop making goo-goo eyes at his girlfriend.

When Shay glanced back at Andi, the other woman was smiling, causing Shay's face to heat. "I feel like a teenager falling for a rockstar. It's like some kinda romance channel movie or something."

Andi laughed and leaned against the counter. "I know what you mean. And I'm not going to interfere in my brother's love life but I have never seen him look at another woman the way he looks at you." Andi seemed to sober then, sneaking a peak at

Rhys. "I honestly thought for a while we were gonna lose him. I didn't think the music was gonna be enough to keep him above ground, and it wasn't. I think he needed more than the music, Shay; he needed you."

Shay felt emotion thicken in her throat and she had to clear it before she could respond. "Rhys was the one who put in the work. He was the one who tried to be better, to do better. You give me too much credit."

"And I think you don't give yourself enough credit. Thank you for loving him even when he couldn't love himself."

Shay wasn't prepared for Andi to embrace her, and it took her by surprise even as she wrapped her arms around the other woman and awkwardly patted her back. Rhys lifted his brows in question as Shay gave him a puzzled look before Andi stepped out of the embrace.

Andi was grinning, and Shay watched as Declan and Andi shared a look, then Declan nodded, and Andi all but dragged Shay over to where Rhys was still talking to Declan. Andi seemed excited as she reached for Declan's hand, leaning into him.

"Go on, tell him...You've been dying to tell him." Declan said with a grin.

Rhys glanced from Declan to Andi and back again. "Jesus, Christ, are you pregnant?"

Declan made a strangled sound as Andi smacked her little brother on the arm. "No, I'm fucking not, you idiot. But I do have a surprise for you. Remember your old piano teacher, Mrs. Canning?"

"Ya, we only talked about her a little while ago," Rhys replied, his hand coming around her waist and pulling Shay closer.

Andi smiled, her face almost giddy as she said. "Well she lives in New York now with her son, and one of her former students is a member of the board of directors for Carnegie Hall, and she emailed me last week to ask if you would be interested in being the main performer for their Irish celebration, where all Irish musicians played a fundraiser for funding for music for underprivileged children."

"So, she wants the band to play a gig for charity?" Rhys asked, and Shay felt his fingers dig into her hip.

"No doofus...just you. She wanted to know if you would fulfil her dream of seeing you play piano in Carnegie Hall. Just you Rhys. When I told her that you had found your voice again, she said that fate had aligned and there was no other musician she wanted to close out the show than you."

Rhys seemed stunned into silence, his entire body tense and when he didn't say anything for the longest time, Andi looked at Declan, almost pleading with him to help him out, but Declan just shook his head as if to say give him time.

"Is she sure she wants just me...I mean, the band would be more of an asset than me on my own."

Andi let go of Declan's hand and reached for Rhys.

"Yes, I'm sure. It's a classical music thing and she asked for you. We will be there, in the audience, for moral support. It's your time to shine, Rhys."

Everyone started to congratulate Rhys and Shay was so excited for this opportunity for him, even if it meant more time away from each other. Shay moved to the side, so the other members of the band could get to him, but Rhys seemed to sense her moving away and he came towards her, a stupid grin on his face.

"You fancy a trip to New York?"

"You want me to come?" She asked, then Rhys cupped her face and kissed her hard.

"Of course I do. No way I'm gonna do this without the woman I love."

Shay felt her heart explode, knowing that everyone in the room had heard Rhys's declaration. She hadn't been looking for Rhys when she had found him, but now that he was hers, she wasn't about to let him go.

"I love you too, Rhys. I love you too."

CHAPTER THIRTY

Rhys

RHYS HAD FELT like he was about to vomit the entire day leading up to his performance. He'd barely slept the night before, tossing and turning in bed and keeping Shay awake, the only thing that could distract him was the heat of her touch, the warmth of her lips, and the deliciousness of her body.

The trip to New York had been filled with laughter and memories, the entire band, their partners, and his parents had travelled over to watch Rhys perform and he still hadn't decided what song he was going to perform. There was barely an hour to go before he went on stage and he had no clue what he was going to play, let alone if he could find the nerve to sing.

"Rhys?"

Rhys glanced up from where he was sat backstage to see an older woman smiling at him brightly. She reached him, then rested a hand on his shoulder as he began to rise, choosing to take a seat beside him.

"It makes an old woman happy to finally see you in the place I always envisioned I would."

"It's nice to see ya again, Mrs. Canning. Thank you for pulling the strings to get me invited."

The older woman grinned, patting his knee. "You were always my most talented student, Rhys. You could hear the music like no one else could."

Rhys shook his head. "Nah, Andi was better than I was."

Mrs. canning frowned at Rhys, shaking her head. "That's nonsense. Your sister was talented, yes, and she didn't try and stray away from the classical like you did, but you had something unique that only a person with a mind like yours could have. It made you special, and tonight, I look forward to watching you see that for yourself. You always had trouble believing in your talent."

His old teacher left him then, citing her need to make sure she had enough time to get to her seat before his performance. Left alone to his own devices, Rhys started to stress again. He couldn't help feeling like a fraud, sitting here in his back suit, shirt, and bow tie. Even his dress shoes pinched and he knew it would just make his performance more uncomfortable.

He still had time to back out right?

"You look like you're about to do a runner."

Rhys chuckled as he glanced up as Declan came to sit beside him, lounging in the seat. "The thought had crossed my mind."

Declan ran his eyes over Rhys. "I don't think I've ever seen you look so formal. It's weird."

"It feels weird. I don't feel like myself." Rhys admitted, leaning forward to rest his elbows on his knees and his chin in his hands.

"Shay said you weren't comfortable in the formal stuff Andi picked out for you. So if you are uncomfortable, Rhys, and you don't feel like yourself, then go out there as you. Go out as Rhys fucking Collins who can stand in front of thousands of people barefoot, dressed in skinny jeans and nothing but a cocky smile. You do you...fuck what anyone else thinks."

Rhys snorted, sighing. "Oh ya, like I can act myself performing by myself in Carnegie Hall. Be serious, Dec."

Declan stood up, then forced Rhys to stand up too, his best friend facing him as Declan reached out and undid the black bowtie, then tossed it aside. He motioned for Rhys to take off the stuffy suit jacket, taking it from him and setting it down on the chair. Rhys rolled up the sleeves of his dress shirt, then Declan proceeded to unbutton the top two buttons.

"While I can't condone stripping all the way off, I think this is all you. But take off the shoes, Rhys. Even a novice like me knows you won't play well in shoes you're not comfortable in."

Rhys laughed as he did what Declan told him, instantly feeling more like himself once he was free of the stuffy suit, although his pants weren't what he would have chosen to wear, but still, he felt more himself now.

"Andi's gonna be pissed," Rhys said as he fidgeted with the sleeves of his shirt, stopping to look at Declan, who smiled and shook his head.

"Nah, Andi won't care. She would just want you to do you and once you're happy, who the fuck cares what anyone else thinks. If you go out there pretending to be someone you're not, and this opportunity passes you by, you'll regret it."

"What if I fuck it up, Dec. What if I just embarrass myself?"

Declan reached out and gripped his shoulder. "You won't. I am so fucking proud of you, Rhys. So damn proud. And so is everyone sitting out there waiting to watch you have your moment in the spotlight. You got this. I love ya, brother."

Declan gave Rhys' shoulder one last squeeze, as Rhys felt his throat tighten, unable to say the words back to Declan, but his friend smiled, inclining his head and Rhys knew that Declan understood. Rhys watched his friend walk away and realized just how much he could have lost if Andi and Declan hadn't forced him to go to that treatment centre.

Had he continued on his self-destructive path, then he might never have been forced to own up to all the stupid shit he had pulled, all the pain he had caused, and him and Declan might never have made amends. He might have shattered his relationship with Andi and missed out on all the things to come.

And then there was Shay. It wasn't until he almost lost her, before he'd even had the chance to love her, had Rhys realized that sometimes love comes along when you aren't looking for it, when you feel broken and torn apart inside until someone special comes along who takes the broken pieces inside you and doesn't try to fix them, but embraces them.

Shay had done that for him and given him a deeper understanding of what love was.

Rhys had been struggling to pick a song that would showcase his talents and up until that very moment, he hadn't even been sure that he was going to try and sing. He remembered laying in bed, watching Shay as she sketched, heard her hum along to the Metallica song that was playing on her playlist, and just how beautiful she had looked.

"You're up next, Mr. Collins."

The attendant's voice dragged him out of his thoughts as Rhys inhaled a breath, hoping to steady his nerves. He waited for his queue to go on stage as he pretended it was just like any other show he had done, and Declan, Jameson, and Luna were all on stage waiting for him.

"Ladies and gentlemen, last but certainly not least, we have an extraordinary young man who we normally see rocking the stage with his band, Heartache Melody, but tonight, he is going to honour us with a very special performance. May I introduce, Rhys Collins."

Rhys waited a moment before he raised his head and strode out on the stage, the applause and whistles, no doubt from his own family and friends so loud that when he sat behind the piano, barefoot and sleeves rolled up, he had to wait for the auditorium to quieten before he could speak into the microphone.

"This is dedicated to Shay Gleeson, the girl who healed my heart."

He cast a glance out into the audience, taking a moment to take in Shay's face, her eyes filled with love as she clasped a hand over her mouth, knowing that the event was being streamed online and now the world would know that Rhys Collins was no longer the party boy of Heartache Melody and Shay had his heart.

The lights dimmed then, and Rhys focused on his moment, playing the first few bars of *Nothing Else Matters*, the version Dermot Kennedy had perfected, then Rhys opened his mouth, his voice and his fingers telling his story, the lyrics flowing from his lips like he had been singing all of his life and Rhys finally knew that this, this was happiness.

When he finished, Rhys closed his eyes for a moment, then slowly got to his feet, turning to face the audience, and then the lights went back on. The entire auditorium got to their feet, clapping, his friends and family the loudest cheerers of all. Rhys looked to where Shay stood beside his sister, her eyes wet with tears, and Rhys fell all over again as his girlfriend mouthed that she loved him, and Rhys blew her a kiss.

His chest ached from his heart being so full and his face hurt from smiling so much as he bowed, then straightened, knowing he would remember this feeling for the rest of his life. He had dove down a dark path alone, only to realize he was loved, he mattered, and that love comes in many different forms...be it the love between two best friends or the unconditional love between siblings.

Sometimes, it came from a sexy tattoo artist who wasn't afraid to call him on his bullshit.

And Rhys wouldn't have it any other way.

THE END

The Rebel County Universe Stories continue in
Best Laid Plans (Rebel Books Book 1)

Find More Rebel Stories On Kindle Vella

Breaking the Habit is the first novel in the Rebel Ink Trilogy. Rebel Ink is part of the Rebel County Universe which will span at least four different businesses, with intersecting timelines, and characters popping up when you least expect them.

The Rebel Racers Trilogy
Available Now:
Adrenaline Junkie (Rebel Racers Book 1)
All or Nothing (Rebel Racers Book 2)
Crash and Burn (Rebel Racers Book 3)

The Rebel Rock Trilogy
Available Now:
Centre Stage (Rebel Rock Book 1)
Strings Attached (Rebel Rock Book 2)
Make or Break (Rebel Rock Book 3)

The Rebel Ink Trilogy
Available Now:
Breaking the Habit (Rebel Ink Book 1)

The Rebel Books Trilogy
Available Now:
Best Laid Plans (Rebel Books Book 1)

Playlists

Rhys

Ed Sheeran - Drunk
Linkin Park - Breaking the Habit
Phantogram - Black Out Days - Sped Up
Ed Sheeran - Bad Habits (feat. Bring Me The Horizon)
Billie Eilish - xanny
grandson - Overdose
Young the Giant - Cough Syrup
The Verve - The Drugs Don't Work
NF - Paralyzed
UPSAHL - Drugs (feat. blackbear)
Fall Out Boy - I Don't Care
Billie Eilish - when the party's over
Nothing But Thieves - Itch
Nothing But Thieves - Soda
Dennis Lloyd - Breakdown

Stereophonics - My Own Worst Enemy
Billie Eilish - TV
You Me At Six - DEEP CUTS
King Princess - I Hate Myself, I Want To Party
Linkin Park – Numb
Bring Me The Horizon - medicine
Muse - Sing for Absolution
The Fray - Be Still
Macklemore & Ryan Lewis - St. Ides
KID BRUNSWICK - Prescription Kid
UPSAHL - People I Don't Like
Nothing But Thieves - Unperson
Des Rocs - Nothing Personal
Robbie Williams - No Regrets
NF - Trauma
Billie Eilish - Six Feet Under
The Verve - The Drugs Don't Work
Linkin Park - In the End
Evanescence - My Immortal
Matchbox Twenty - Unwell - 2007 Remaster
Bring Me The Horizon - Doomed
Harry Styles - Sign of the Times
Pierce The Veil - Pass The Nirvana
Imagine Dragons - I Don't Like Myself
The Band CAMINO - 1 Last Cigarette
YUNGBLUD - casual sabotage
Måneskin - THE LONELIEST
Dermot Kennedy - Nothing Else Matters
Frank Carter & The Rattlesnakes - The Drugs

SHAY

Jax Jones - Lonely Heart

Arctic Monkeys - Why'd You Only Call Me When You're High?

Tove Lo - Habits (Stay High)

The Weeknd - Can't Feel My Face

Eminem - Won't Back Down

Fall Out Boy - Novocaine

Panic! At The Disco - Don't Threaten Me with a Good Time

Nothing But Thieves - Painkiller

P!nk - Irrelevant

The Stickmen Project - Tears In Ibiza (feat. AR/CO)

Ruelle - Self Sabotage

Macklemore - CHANT (feat. Tones And I)

Craig David - DNA

Russ - Are You Entertained (feat. Ed Sheeran)

Tom Grennan - All These Nights

Bad Suns - Maybe You Saved Me

YUNGBLUD - The Emperor

Paramore - Ain't It Fun

Tom Odell - Heal

Bea Miller - i can't breathe

Isak Danielson - Believe

Paramore - Decode - Acoustic Version

Evanescence - Good Enough

Limp Bizkit - Boiler

MOTHICA - r.e.m. - lofi

RAYE - Black Mascara.

YUNGBLUD - Don't Feel Like Feeling Sad Today

NF - My Stress

My Chemical Romance - Welcome to the Black Parade

Dermot Kennedy - Heartless - Recorded At RAK Studios, London

NOTHING MORE - YOU DON'T KNOW WHAT LOVE MEANS

Panic! At The Disco - Nicotine

poutyface - Rag Doll

Sleeping With Sirens - Let You Down (feat. Charlotte Sands)

blackbear - toxic energy (with Bert McCracken of The Used)

Maggie Lindemann - you're not special

Hot Milk - I Fell in Love With Someone I Shouldn't Have

MOTHICA - LAST CIGARETTE (feat. Au/Ra)

Dermot Kennedy - Kiss Me

Marcus Mumford - Ted Lasso Theme

Tom Ford - The Devil Always Gets Her Way

Man-Made Sunshine - Life's Gonna Kill You (If You Let It)

RAYE - Escapism.

Sleeping With Sirens - Be Happy (feat. Royal & the Serpent)

Acknowledgments

None of this would be possible without an amazing team supporting me! Many thanks to:

Publishing House: CTP Publishing
Cover design: Gem Promotions
Interior Formating: Gem Promotions

———

And as always:
Thank you to all the readers!
Whether this is your first book by me or you've been with me for years! I only get to do this because of you, and I am eternally grateful to each and every one of you who took a chance on this Irish author.

About the Author

Susan Harris is a writer from Cork, Ireland and when she's not torturing her readers with heart-wrenching plot twists or killer cliffhangers, she's probably getting some new book related ink, binging her latest TV or music obsession, or with her nose in a book.

Susan LOVES connecting with her fans!
www.susanharrisauthor.com

Also by Susan Harris

The Wings Of Deceit Series

Angel's Gambit, book 1

Angel's Rebel, book 2

The Ever Chace Chronicles

Skin & Bones, book 1

Collateral Damage, book 2

Smoke & Mirrors, book 3

Night of the Hunter, book 4

Never Back Down, book 5

Shortcut to the Grave, book 6

Arsonist's Lullaby, book 7

Of Gods & Monsters, book 8

————

Shattered Memories

————

Defy The Stars

A Tale of Two Houses, book 1

Until Death Do Us Part, book 2

In Defiance of the Stars, book 3

Courting Darkness, a novella

The Sanguine Crown

Chaos Theory, book 1

Butterfly Effect, book 2

Wicked Game, book 3

Burn Notice, book 4

Fight Song, book 5

The Sicarius Security Series

Kiss Of Death, book 1

Leap Of Faith, book 2

Visions Of Destiny, book 3

War Of Hearts, book 4

Flames Of Conflict, book 5

Why does the wrong guy feel so right?

I had my perfect husband all picked out, but then he decided to marry someone else. So, on the night of his engagement party, I'm drowning my sorrows with my BFF Kari ... and in walks Mitchell Cole.

Mitch is the slow-talking, sexy-walking, eye-crinkle-having star of one of Kari's soap operas, but he doesn't do a thing for me. I need a career guy with a steady job and a plan, not a scruffy actor who works construction between gigs.

Then Kari "volunteers" me to hang out with him so I can get behind-the-scenes gossip for her. And that's all it is, even if his special blend of sweet and sexy is starting to break through my defenses.

But then my ex comes back into my life in the most unexpected way, and that's when things get confusing. Do I choose the man who's everything I thought I wanted? Or the man who might be everything I need?